When drifter Mulvane rides from the high country
into B   he
middle   1's
sheep   oth
want   on,
who's   But
when   gn-
ment   ay
from   he
beauti   vs,
howev   at
isn't h   ose
side t   ed
when   he
back,   —
wonde   ght
betwe

MULVANE'S WAR

WILLIAM HEUMAN

SAGEBRUSH
Large Print Westerns

First published in the United States by Avon Books

First Isis Edition
published 2019
by arrangement with
Golden West Literary Agency

A catalogue record for this book is available
from the British Library.

ISBN 978–1–78541–682–8 (pb)

Published by
F. A. Thorpe (Publishing)
Anstey, Leicestershire

Set by Words & Graphics Ltd.
Anstey, Leicestershire
Printed and bound in Great Britain by
T. J. International Ltd., Padstow, Cornwall

CHAPTER
ONE

The little blue coffeepot was not an expensive one, but sentiment was attached to it. Mulvane had carried it about with him for eight years, and it had made him many a cup of excellent coffee on raw, wintry mornings or chill evenings in high valleys like this one. Now, with bullet holes drilled through both sides of it, two inches up from the bottom, and lying on its side in the dust, the brew spilled out, it would never be used again.

Aside from the sentiment, Mulvane did not like to have a hidden rifleman send a slug whistling through his coffeepot as he made his noonday meal. It had been rough crossing the ten-thousand-foot Owl Head Pass, and now, having descended here to the timberline, Mulvane was tired and hungry.

The claybank gelding he had been riding had moved down another fifty feet, and was grazing in a tiny park. The animal had lifted its head, snorting nervously at the sound of the rifle shot. Mulvane, at the fire, had not moved an inch. He sat there with his back against the tree, a fairly tall man with hard gray eyes and Indian-black hair, his wide, thin-lipped mouth creased in a frown.

There was a Winchester rifle in the saddle holster on the claybank, and Mulvane carried a Colt .45 on his right hip, but he made no attempt to go for either gun. The rifleman off in the brush had him covered neatly and cleanly; that shot had been fired to apprise him of the fact.

Keeping his hands high, Mulvane took cigarette papers and the packet of Bull Durham from his shirt pocket and unhurriedly rolled himself a smoke. Then he put the cigarette in his mouth and touched a match to it, breaking the match in half before tossing it into the fire.

He had not as yet turned his head in the direction from which the shot had come. Sitting there, smoking the cigarette, he heard movement off to his left and the sound of someone else coming toward him from the right. He continued to stare into the fire, the frown still on his face. The coffeepot had been a cheap one, and he could pick up another in the next town for less than a dollar, but he'd liked that pot.

The man coming toward him from the left said caustically, "Keep your hands away from that gun, Jack."

Mulvane had drawn up his legs, and his arms were resting on his knees now as he sat facing the fire. He turned his head, however, to look at the man coming toward him through the trees. The rifleman was still carrying his Remington rifle in one hand, but he had a pistol in the other as he came around the fire.

He was tall and bony, with sand-colored hair, and tough, pale blue eyes. His nose had been broken, and

2

was twisted slightly to the left. He wore a scuffed, brown leather jacket and a black Stetson with the rim broken.

Mulvane looked at him, no expression on his face, realizing that he was caught here in a bind. The second man was coming toward him from the opposite direction, and he, too, undoubtedly had a gun in hand, and was ready to use it.

"Take off the gunbelt, mister," the tall one snapped.

Mulvane looked at him for a moment and then leisurely unbuckled the gunbelt, tossing it aside. The second man came out of the brush now, a shorter man with small, squinting eyes the color of green glass. He, too, was carrying a Remington rifle, and he had a big Navy Colt in the holster at his side.

Mulvane looked from one to the other, and a faint, cold smile broke over his face. He said softly, "Reckon you boys are loaded for bear."

The little fellow said with a grin, "Kick him in the face, Reese. Then he won't talk so much with his mouth."

Reese grinned, too, revealing yellowish teeth. He said, "Just ride in over the pass?"

Mulvane nodded, and then he looked at the coffeepot on the ground and said, "Reckon you boys owe me for a new pot."

Reese said softly, "We'll owe you a lot more, mister, before we're finished with you."

"Will you?" Mulvane said, still sitting with his back against the tree, as the shorter man stepped up to pick up the gunbelt from the ground.

Reese said to the shorter man, "See that he ain't got a knife on him, Ed."

"You have four guns on me," Mulvane said, and smiled. "You worried about a damned knife?" Then he nodded toward a hunting knife he'd stuck into the ground, near one of the rocks around his fire, that he'd intended to use to roast his bacon.

Ed picked up the knife, looked at it for a moment and then threw it into the tree a few inches above Mulvane's head. Mulvane sat there, looking up at him, and then he said easily, "You could have missed, mister."

"An' you could be dead," Ed told him. "Who would care either way?"

Mulvane just shrugged. He looked up at Reese, who was covering him with the pistol, and said, "Your job in this country to go around shooting up coffeepots?"

The grin on Reese's bony face broadened. He said simply, "Work on him, Ed."

Mulvane was not prepared for what happened next. When Reese spoke, Ed stepped forward swiftly and crashed the barrel of his six-gun across Mulvane's hat.

Mulvane tried to raise his right arm to ward off the blow, but he was only partly successful. Stunned, he felt himself falling over on his side. As he fell, Ed slashed at his head with the gun barrel again.

Just partly conscious now, he heard Reese say viciously, "The boot now, Tolivar."

Something collided with Mulvane's left cheekbone, and he knew that he'd been kicked brutally in the face.

4

He felt the blood trickle down from the gash on his cheekbone.

He tried to rise to his feet, but the boot caught him again, this time on the side of the jaw. He sprawled forward on his face, anger raging in him.

Mulvane was aware of a few more kicks in the body and around the head. Then he heard a girl's voice, sharp, vibrant with anger, and the kicking stopped.

As though from a long way off, he heard the girl say, "I want some water brought here."

Rolling over, Mulvane managed to come to a sitting position. His face was throbbing with pain, and there was a sharp ache in his right side that he hoped wasn't a cracked rib.

When his eyes came into focus clearly, he could see a girl standing on the other side of the fire, looking down at him. She was of medium height and wore worn blue levis, a black-and-red checked flannel shirt and a black leather jacket.

Mulvane's gaze was arrested by her hair, the lightest blonde hair he'd ever seen in his life — almost white, beautiful, fine like spun gold. It was combed back away from her face and pulled up in a knot at the back. She had a small, upturned nose and a rather straight but not unwomanly mouth. Her eyes were blue and blazing with anger now as she watched the short man, Ed, come back from the pool carrying the perforated coffeepot and trying to stop the water trickling from the two holes.

"How do you feel now?" she asked, turning to Mulvane.

Mulvane looked at Reese, standing a few yards away, and then at Ed, who was handing him the coffeepot, and said softly, "Reckon I owe these boys something, ma'am."

Reese said, "He rode in over the pass, Miss McSween, an' we got orders from your father to turn 'em back, every one of 'em."

"Are you supposed to kill them?" the girl snapped at him.

"Reckon we wasn't killin' him," Reese said, grinning. "Just puttin' the fear in him, ma'am."

Mulvane took the coffeepot, drank some of the cold water from it and then splashed more water into his face. He spotted a chestnut mare standing at the edge of the clearing and figured that it belonged to the girl.

Reese was saying, "Reckon we ought to find out who he is, Miss McSween. Your father won't like it if we let him ride past. You know how he is about such things."

The girl said to Mulvane, "Were you hired by Boyd Harmon?"

Mulvane tossed the coffeepot to one side and rose to his feet, dabbing at his bleeding face with a moistened bandanna. "Who's Boyd Harmon?" he asked.

"He's lyin' like hell," Ed Tolivar said.

Mulvane rubbed his hands on his pants. He said, "You want to hand me back that gun and then say it again, mister?"

Ed said glumly, "All of 'em talk tough, an' all of 'em lie like hell."

Miss McSween repeated, "You didn't come here to work for Boyd Harmon down on the lowlands?"

Mulvane shook his head. "Never heard of Harmon," he repeated.

Reese scowled. "Have to take him down to see your father. I ain't lettin' him ride through an' then have to take a tongue-lashin' from Jehu McSween."

Ed brought up the claybank, and the girl said to Mulvane, "I think you'd better follow us."

Mulvane put one hand on the saddle. "You the law around here, ma'am?" he said, smiling.

"There's not much law up here near the timber-line," the girl told him quietly. "We have to make our own."

Ed was carrying Mulvane's gunbelt, and Reese had slipped Mulvane's Winchester from the saddle holster. Unarmed, he stepped into the saddle and followed the girl as she rode on ahead of him downgrade, with Reese and Ed coming along behind them.

Reese called up to him once, "We got a gun on you, mister. Don't forget that."

Mulvane turned his head slightly. His head and body were throbbing from the beating he'd taken from these two men, and he said softly, "I won't forget it, mister. Reckon I'll remember you."

7

CHAPTER
TWO

The four of them rode another half mile or so down the mountainside. Then Mulvane's nose wrinkled as he caught the rank odor of sheep. Minutes later he saw a big flock of them feeding in a meadow off to his right.

As he skirted the meadow a half dozen yards behind Miss McSween, he saw her lift a hand to the herder with the sheep. The man, a short, blocky, dark-skinned fellow, waved back. A dog came at them, barking furiously, then gave up and trotted back toward the herder's wagon.

Mulvane said to the girl up ahead, "Boyd Harmon a cattleman?"

Miss McSween looked back at him. "Mr. Harmon runs stock down on the lower range," she said.

Mulvane immediately realized what the situation was here in this high hill country. This was another sheepherder-cattleman war, and both sides were probably bringing in gunsharps to protect their rights. This hill country was broken up with small, lush valleys, ideal for sheep raising, and Mulvane knew very well that cattlemen also liked these high, grassy meadows for summer grazing and for fattening up stock before shipping East.

8

They were moving down a winding trail that led away from the meadow in which the sheep had been grazing. As a westerly breeze blew the odor of the sheep in their direction, Mulvane wrinkled his nose in disgust. Like all men born and raised on the open range, he despised sheep.

Now they were approaching a house that had been built into the side of the hill. The house, made of split logs, was quite large. It was long and L-shaped, consisting of at least five rooms, with horse sheds in the rear.

White wood-smoke was curling up from a chimney at one end of the house, and, as the four riders approached, a man came out and stood on the veranda, which overlooked a mile-long valley below the house.

Mulvane stared in amazement at the man on the veranda. He was huge, possibly weighing close to three hundred pounds and he was inches over six feet tall. He had a heavy black beard and tremendous hamlike hands, the thumbs of which were hooked into his belt.

The big man on the veranda spoke in a booming voice, his intense blue eyes fixed upon Mulvane, who had pulled up the claybank just below him. "Who in hell is this?" he asked.

"Gunsharp Boyd Harmon brought in here," Reese said. "Figured you'd like to see him, Mr. McSween."

The girl said quickly, "We don't know that he's riding for the cattlemen, Father. Beemish and Tolivar jumped his camp back up toward the pass. He claims he doesn't know Harmon."

McSween said to Reese Beemish, "You figured he was a Harmon rider, Beemish?"

Beemish grinned. "Damn well looks like one."

McSween said reflectively, "Kind of worked him over, too, didn't you? Even when you weren't sure."

Little Ed Tolivar chuckled. "We weren't takin' any chances. You start askin' these boys questions, Mr. McSween, an you're dead. Reckon you know that."

McSween nodded. He looked again at Mulvane, who was sitting loosely in the saddle, listening but saying nothing. McSween snapped at him, "Speak up, man. Boyd Harmon bring you in here to gun down our herders?"

Mulvane took his time before replying. He looked the giant straight in the eye and said, "I never heard of any damned Boyd Harmon. I rode in over the pass at noon, and these two dogs jumped my camp."

McSween grinned, revealing a set of very white teeth through the black beard. "Reckon you could be lying like hell, mister," he said. "Where were you heading when you came in over Owl Head?"

"Everybody asks a hell of a lot of questions in this country," Mulvane said. "I was heading where my horse took me. That answer your question?"

McSween nodded. "A drifter," he said. "Maybe you'd like to ride for me, mister, if you're not riding for Boyd Harmon."

Mulvane shook his head. "I don't like the smell of sheep," he said, "and I wouldn't share a bunkhouse with a pair of skunks." He looked straight at Beemish and Tolivar.

10

"You're talkin' pretty big with your mouth now, mister," Beemish said grimly. "We could work on you some more with the barrel of this gun."

McSween said, "If we let you go, you aim to join up with Boyd Harmon?"

"None of your damned business," Mulvane said, and he saw the grin spread across McSween's face again.

McSween chuckled. "Easiest way to take care of you is to put a bullet in the back of your head and drop you into a pothole somewhere. Then you wouldn't join anybody. How about that, now?"

Mulvane smiled. "You have the guns," he said, aware that the flaxen-haired girl was watching him.

Beemish and Tolivar had dismounted, but Mulvane was still sitting in the saddle, arms folded across his chest, looking up at McSween. Now he knew how, and why, the sheepherders in this country had become so strong that they were now bucking the cattlemen with their own gunhands.

McSween was evidently a man who made decisions in a hurry. He said, "You don't want to ride for us, mister, you won't ride for Harmon, either. You know what's best for you, you'll ride to hell out of here and keep going. Give him his gun, Beemish."

Reese Beemish took Mulvane's gunbelt from his saddle and walked reluctantly over with it.

"Give it to him," McSween roared, "and step lively, man!"

Beemish handed Mulvane the gunbelt, and Mulvane strapped it on.

"What's your damned name?" McSween asked.

"They call me Mulvane," he said.

McSween lifted his eyebrows slightly. "Heard about a tough named Mulvane put the fear in a bunch of damned nesters up in the Sulphur Hills country."

Mulvane didn't answer. He watched Reese Beemish and Ed Tolivar lead their horses up toward the horse sheds, and then he stepped down from the saddle.

"Hold it up," Mulvane said sharply.

The McSween riders stopped and turned to look at him, and Jehu McSween watched him curiously.

"What in hell you want?" Beemish asked.

Mulvane moved away from the claybank. He said softly, "You boys were pretty rough back up near the pass when you had all the guns. Let's see how you make out now."

The two men stared at him, and the left side of Beemish's mouth began to twitch nervously. Beemish looked over at Tolivar, and then he said gruffly, "You callin' us, mister?"

Mulvane nodded. "I'm calling you. Move away from the horse."

McSween stood on the veranda, looking down at them silently. Mulvane noticed that the girl was looking up at her father as though she expected him to stop the coming fight. McSween said only, "Charity, get to hell up on the veranda."

Beemish was not too anxious for a fight. He looked at Ed Tolivar again and rubbed his hands on the sides of his pants. "You're askin' for a hell of a lot of trouble, mister," he growled.

12

Mulvane smiled. "Move away from the horse and quit talking," he said.

Tolivar began to move closer toward the house, separating himself from Beemish. This meant that, when the lead started to fly, it would be coming from different directions and Mulvane would have a hard time covering both guns.

Beemish did not want to fight, but the odds of two guns against one weren't too bad. He licked his lips and looked at Mulvane steadily, but he still didn't make his first move.

As Tolivar edged closer toward the house, Jehu McSween spoke from the veranda, his voice flat and unemotional. "You're out of it, Tolivar," he said. "Sit down on that step."

Tolivar scowled, and Reese Beemish was visibly shaken.

"Sit down," McSween roared, and Tolivar obediently sat down on the bottom step.

"Hell," Beemish mumbled. "You ain't lettin' this gunsharp push us around, are you, Mr. McSween?"

"Reckon you did your share of pushing back up the mountain," McSween told him. "Now push some more if you got the guts."

Beemish looked at him, hatred coming into his pale blue eyes, and then he looked at the man standing less than a dozen yards away. Beemish had had two guns before, and now he had only one — and he, too, had heard of a man called Mulvane.

Mulvane said, "You shot the hell out of my coffeepot back up the hill, mister. You owe me four bits for that.

You're too yellow to fight, so crawl up here with the four bits and pay off."

"You're crazy," Beemish said. "Reckon we made a mistake figurin' you was ridin' for Harmon. I'll pay for the damned pot." He put a hand in his levis pocket and came out with some change, and then he started forward as though he were going to hand the money to Mulvane. He stopped when he saw the gun lined on him.

"What the hell!" he spluttered. He'd been watching those cold eyes, and hadn't even seen the man's hand move.

"You hear good," Mulvane said gently. "I told you to *crawl*, mister, on hands and knees."

Reese Beemish stared at him in disbelief. "You're crazy," he said shrilly.

Mulvane put the gun back into the holster. "Crawl," he said, "or draw that gun — one or the other."

Mulvane started to walk forward then, very slowly. He stopped when he was less than ten feet away from his man.

"I'm payin' you the damned money." Beemish scowled, his face a mottled color. "I'm payin', ain't I?"

Mulvane, his face still throbbing and hurting from the beating he'd taken from these two men, shook his head. "Not enough. Get down on your knees, mister."

"Hell with you," Beemish said, choking. He had the coins in his hand, but he couldn't bring himself to go down on his knees.

Mulvane walked forward again, taking his time, watching Beemish's gun hand, even though he was positive now that the man was past the fighting stage. Reese Beemish did not wish to die.

When Mulvane was within arm's reach of the man, he slipped the gun from Beemish's holster and tossed it aside. He said, "Pay me the four bits, mister."

Beemish's mouth was twitching violently now. He handed Mulvane the coins without a word, and Mulvane dropped them in his pocket. Then he lashed out with his right hand, striking Beemish full across the face as hard as he could with an open-hand slap. He slapped him four more times, back and forth. They were hard, heavy blows, and Beemish staggered, nearly falling, and cursed as he stumbled away.

Mulvane turned then and looked at Tolivar, still sitting on the lower step of the veranda. He said, "How about you, mister?"

The short man didn't say anything. His greenish eyes were half closed as he watched Mulvane come up to him.

Mulvane smiled. "You had a rifle and a pistol up in the hills. You still have a pistol. Like to see if it works?"

Tolivar still didn't say anything, and Mulvane walked up to him casually and smiled.

"You're not fighting today," he said, "only kicking — at a man who is down on the ground without a gun. That the way it is, Tolivar?"

Tolivar looked at Mulvane and then away, and Mulvane hit him an open-handed blow across the face, sending him sprawling into the dust.

Tolivar rolled and came up in a sitting position. Mulvane said, "You still have your gun, mister."

Ed Tolivar was frozen, but there was boiling hatred in his eyes.

Mulvane turned his back on both men, knowing that they wouldn't go for their guns in front of McSween. They would undoubtedly come after him again if he stayed in this country, but never from the front.

Stepping into the saddle, he nodded up at Jehu McSween, who was looking down at him from the veranda, respect in his blue eyes.

"You'll never whip Harmon with a crew like that," Mulvane said, smiling. "Why don't you hire some men, McSween?"

"I made an offer to you," McSween said.

Mulvane chuckled. "Sheep stink, and to hell with them."

The girl was watching him as he started to ride off, and he thought idly that, if it had been cattle instead of sheep, this would have been as nice a place as any to hole up for a while — until he decided to cross the next mountain.

CHAPTER
THREE

The little town of Boulder City nestled in the foothills of the high mountains over which Mulvane had just come. It was a small town, but apparently prospering. With both cattlemen and sheepherders in the area, and with both seemingly doing well, it was a good town for business. New buildings and stores were going up along the single main street even as Mulvane rode in.

The town had the usual hotel, a number of saloons and, beyond the hotel, a new livery stable, just finished and being painted. Mulvane turned in under the arch leading up to the stable. It was late afternoon now. He'd left the McSween place about two hours earlier, and he hadn't had his noonday meal yet.

He'd been on the move for more than a week now, sleeping in his blankets on the ground, and he felt the need of a hotel bed, a hot bath and a haircut. First of all, though, he wanted to eat.

Leaving the claybank with the livery man, he stepped into the restaurant nearby, ordered a steak and eggs and waited impatiently until the food came.

He ate unhurriedly. The steak was good, rare, and with side orders of onions and fried potatoes. He had apple pie with coffee after the steak, and then he sat at the table for some time and smoked a cigar before getting up and crossing to the hotel.

Since he'd come into town, he had been aware that people were watching him carefully. He knew these hills were full of gunslingers, and undoubtedly the townspeople were wondering which side he was on.

Registering at the hotel, he went up to his room with his warbag, took out a clean shirt and clean levis and changed into them. Then he came down and crossed to the barber shop, which had a sign on the window indicating that a hot bath could be had for two bits.

The barber was a short, dapper man with a neatly trimmed black mustache. As he draped the apron around Mulvane's neck he said, "Just ride in?"

"Just rode in," Mulvane answered.

The little barber started to clip his hair. "You had your supper over at Miller's Restaurant, and you registered at the Boulder City Hotel," he said. "That could mean that you're not riding for Boyd Harmon. If you were, you could be out at Circle H and saving yourself room rent at the hotel. On the other hand, you might be looking for Harmon."

Mulvane said, "You see a lot, barber."

"I stand here all day." The barber grinned. "What else is there to do? A man can get damned sick of cutting hair."

Mulvane smiled. "I came here to have mine cut, not to hear you talk."

"Any way you want it." The barber paused for one last question: "You a McSween man?"

"No," Mulvane said. "Now cut hair."

The barber didn't ask any more questions, and Mulvane was quite sure the little man had assumed he was a McSween rider despite his denial.

After the haircut and shave, Mulvane took a bath in the galvanized tub at the rear of the barber shop. The hot water felt good, and he lay in it for some time, letting the soreness ease out of his body.

When he came back into the shop to pay his bill, the barber was waiting. "Figured you might like to know, mister. Boyd Harmon just rode in."

Mulvane shrugged. "Let him ride out again," he said. He paid for his haircut and bath and stepped out into the street.

It was fully dark now, and a rather warm evening. Mulvane remembered that that morning he'd come through a light snow up in Owl Head Pass. Thinking of the Pass reminded him that his face was still sore and swollen around the cheekbone.

He moved down the street, feeling the need of a drink. There were four saloons in this town, two on each side, and he picked the one closest to the hotel. It was called the Cattleman's Bar, and it seemed considerably larger than the other three.

As he pushed in through the bat-wing doors he thought wryly that, if any of the other saloons were sheepmen's bars, he preferred this one. The saloon was fairly crowded, but with plenty of room up at the bar. As he walked past a number of card tables he saw men looking at him again.

The bartender, a fat-faced man with a thick, handlebar mustache, banged a bottle down in front of him with unnecessary violence, then picked up a shot glass and slid it down toward Mulvane, banging it into the bottle.

Mulvane looked at the man, seeing the surly scowl on his face, and realized now that he was being served here with reluctance. The bartender returned his look brazenly, and Mulvane said, "Easy, mister."

He picked up the glass and held it to the light, then slid it back across the bar. He said softly, "Another glass, bartender."

"What the hell's wrong with that one?" the bartender snapped.

"It's dirty," Mulvane told him, smiling.

The bartender slid the glass back, banging it into the bottle again. "Reckon that'll do you, mister," he said tersely.

Mulvane picked up the glass and looked at it. This was a small town, and talk got around it pretty quickly. The little barber had undoubtedly passed the word on that the stranger was not a Harmon man, which meant only one thing — he was a McSween man, and therefore he was in the wrong place for his drink.

Mulvane leaned over the bar, with the glass in his hand, and smashed it hard on the floor on the other side. He said, "Reckon you won't have to wash that one any more, mister. Now get me a clean glass."

Conversation in the saloon had stopped entirely. The drinkers along the bar had turned, and were watching him unsmilingly.

"You'll pay for that glass," the bartender grated, "or you'll get another one rammed down your throat."

20

"Will I?" Mulvane said, and he picked up the bottle in front of him and held it in his right hand. Behind the bar was a long, expensive mirror. Drawing back his arm, he grinned and said, "You like to see that mirror smashed, too, bartender?"

The bartender looked at him as he wiped his hands with a damp cloth. Then he said over his shoulder, "John."

Mulvane watched a big, heavy-shouldered man in a brown derby hat step out of a rear gambling room and move down along the bar.

The bartender said, "Throw that damned sheepman out, John."

John said, grinning, "Over the doors?"

"There's four bits in it," the bartender said, "if you get him over the doors without making them move."

John chuckled. "A pleasure." He was several inches taller than Mulvane, with reddish-brown hair and a wide, bony, scarred face.

Still holding the bottle in his hand, grasping it by the neck, Mulvane leaned back against the bar, watching, a smile on his face.

"Take him," the bartender said.

The floorman had pulled up in front of Mulvane, and was standing with his hands on his hips, the brown derby hat perched on the side of his head. He wore a black suit that was too small for him, short at the cuffs and ankles.

John said, "I've been asked to throw you out, mister. You gonna make it hard for me?"

Mulvane continued to smile at him. He held the liquor bottle loosely and hefted it a few times, watching John's eyes until the floorman switched his gaze to the bottle. Mulvane had been waiting for this, and he lunged forward now, smashing the big floorman squarely in the stomach with his left fist and packing one hundred and eighty pounds behind the blow.

John let out a big *whoosh* and doubled over, his derby hat falling from his head. Almost before the hat reached the floor, Mulvane had swung the bottle, without too much force, against the back of the big fellow's head.

The floorman stumbled, clutching his stomach. He would have fallen, but Mulvane stepped forward to grasp him by the shoulders and push him gently into an empty chair near one of the card tables. John sat there, still doubled up, his head toward the floor, gasping for air.

Mulvane turned to the bartender then and said, "I'll take that glass, mister, and it had better be clean this time."

The bartender pushed a glass toward him without a word, and Mulvane poured some of the liquor out of the bottle with which he'd hit the floorman. Then he turned to look at the big fellow and said to the bartender, "Another glass, mister."

The bartender gave him the glass, and he filled it, stepped over to the card table and placed it on the table beside John. Then he paid for the two drinks, gulped his down and walked toward the door. Every man in the room watched him but no one said anything.

22

Out on the porch he stopped to make a smoke. As he was doing so he heard the doors squeak behind him, and a man came out and stood against the porch pillar opposite him. He was a chunky, blocky man with a barrel chest, and he wore a leather vest.

He watched Cass touch a match to the cigarette, then said, "A McSween man?"

Mulvane looked at him wryly, thinking that the people in this town asked a hell of a lot of questions. "Who are you?" he asked.

The short man grinned. "Griff Bannerman," he stated. "I ramrod for Boyd Harmon. Reckon you went into the wrong place tonight, mister, if you're a McSween man."

Mulvane turned his face toward the light from the interior of the saloon. He pointed to his swollen cheekbone and the cuts, and he said, "McSween men gave me this back up in the hills."

Bannerman nodded. "Figured you weren't a McSween man," he said. "Reckon Boyd Harmon would like to see you, mister. He's over at the hotel now."

Mulvane looked up at the night sky. "Everybody in this damned country has a job for me," he said wryly.

Bannerman shrugged. "Figured if you were just ridin' through you'd like to know that Harmon's paying big money for fast guns. Reckon I'd see him if I were you."

"You're not me," Mulvane reminded him, and he walked off.

Back in the hotel lobby he picked up the local newspaper and sat down in a corner, not wanting to go to his room yet.

He was still sitting there, some thirty minutes later, when the law of Boulder City came into the lobby.

Another one! Mulvane thought, and he lowered the paper, a half grin coming to his face.

The sheriff of Boulder City was a rather frail man. Bony and gray-haired, his shoulders bent, he was a man who seemed to be carrying a burden on him. There were deep lines in his face and around his faded eyes.

Mulvane watched the man over the top of the newspaper as he crossed the lobby. He stopped in front of Mulvane's chair. Mulvane put the newspaper down in his lap and looked up. He grinned and said, "I'm not for McSween, and I'm not for Harmon. That what you want to know, Sheriff?"

A faint, tired smile slid across the lawman's face. He pulled up a chair and sat down across from Mulvane, handing him a cigar. He said, "The name's Rog Denton." Then he touched the star on his faded gray vest as though to further identify himself. "Hear you did a job on John Fogarty," he added.

"How is he?" Mulvane asked.

Sheriff Denton shrugged. "John will have a headache tomorrow," he said. "Reckon that's about all. He's got a pretty hard head."

"That was a hard bottle, too," Mulvane observed, and he put the cigar in his shirt pocket for smoking later.

"So you're not McSween." Denton smiled. "And you're not Harmon. That makes you an ordinary human being, and I'm damned glad to meet you. Haven't met too many lately."

"They making it tough for you?" Mulvane asked.

"No killings, yet," Denton said, scowling. "Two men shot up, some stock stampeded by McSween's toughs and a few hundred head of sheep run over a cliff wall — which is not too much loss, you might say. I don't care a damn for sheep, but those herders have been up in the hills for seven or eight years now, and I reckon they got their rights, too."

Mulvane nodded. "Ran across Jehu McSween when I came over the pass," he said. "They won't push him."

"They won't," Rog Denton agreed. "He's a rough one. He try to sign you up?"

Mulvane nodded.

"Bannerman didn't sign you up, and Harmon didn't sign you up," Rog Denton observed, "so maybe I'll try."

Mulvane's grin broadened. "Damnedest town for wanting a man to work," he said.

"Been trying to line up a few deputies," Denton told him. "Reckon you know how tough it is, the way things are in this town now. The pay is a hundred a month and board, but it's not too damned likely that you'll live a month to collect your first pay."

Mulvane looked at the sheriff and said, laughing, "The pay doesn't interest me, Sheriff. I can get three or four times that much from either Harmon or McSween."

Denton nodded glumly. "Figured I'd ask," he said. "No harm in asking." He added, "If you're not signing with anybody, my advice to you is to ride to hell out of here in the morning. A man caught in the middle of a battle like this isn't in a healthy spot."

Mulvane nodded. "Obliged for the advice. I was mistaken for a Harmon man up in the hills, and they thought I was a McSween man in the Cattleman's Bar. Now, I reckon they'll all figure I work for the law after seeing you!"

Rog Denton laughed and shook his head. As they sat there in the lobby, Mulvane saw a man coming down the stairs from the second floor, a big fellow, solid in the shoulders and trim in the waist, with pale blond hair and green eyes. Like most men in this town he carried a gun, but it was on the left side, and he carried it like a man who knew how to use it.

Crossing the lobby, he lifted a hand to Rog Denton, let his eyes rest upon Mulvane for a moment and then kept going toward the street.

"That's one of 'em," Denton said.

"Harmon?" Mulvane asked.

Denton nodded. "That's him. His father was the first rancher in these parts. He was a tough one, and Boyd is following in his steps."

He stood up, then, looking down at Mulvane. He said, "Any time you change your mind, Mulvane, you'll know where to find me. Hundred a month and board."

Mulvane smiled. "Four or five hundred, and I might think twice, Sheriff. I die for the high dollar."

"They pay me a hundred and fifty to wear this star," Denton said. "All I'm allowed is a hundred a month for deputies, and I can't get a damned one."

Mulvane grinned. "Luck," he said.

Denton took the cigar from his mouth and looked at it. "Might still be plenty of people in this town figure

26

you're a McSween rider hanging around to see if you can learn what Harmon and the others have up their sleeves. I'd walk careful."

Mulvane's smile broadened.

"Damned thing is," Denton added thoughtfully, "you *could* be a McSween man, for all I know."

He shook his head in disgust and left Mulvane sitting in his chair in the lobby, a wide grin on his face.

CHAPTER
FOUR

After Sheriff Denton had gone, Mulvane stepped out onto the porch of the hotel, moved over to a wicker chair in one corner and sat down. He had put a match to the cigar Denton had given him and was enjoying the rich aroma when he spotted Boyd Harmon coming out of the Cattleman's Bar and heading back toward the hotel. Harmon had to pass by him to reach the door of the hotel, and, when he saw Mulvane on the porch, the big rancher slowed down.

Harmon stopped and said tersely, "You the new rooster rode in?"

Cass took the cigar from his mouth. "The name's Mulvane," he said, smiling, "and you didn't sign me up, Harmon."

Harmon nodded, looking at him over the porch rail. He said, "Bannerman couldn't sign you up, either, could he?"

"Reckon not," Mulvane agreed.

"Here's hoping that McSween hasn't signed you up," Boyd Harmon said quietly. "That's for your own good, Mulvane."

"If he'd signed me up, you think I'd be afraid to tell you?"

28

Harmon looked at him. "You're not riding for anybody, mister, so walk easy, and keep out of trouble."

Mulvane said softly, "I walk as I damned please."

Harmon's wide face was in the shadows, but Mulvane sensed the displeasure in it. But all Harmon said, before he walked on, was, "We've had tough ones in these hills before, Mulvane."

"And I've been in tough hills before, too," Mulvane observed.

Watching Harmon walk by and enter the hotel, Mulvane thought to himself that now he knew all of them. He wasn't ready to pick a winner, either. McSween was tough, and Boyd Harmon had the cut of a man who stood on his own feet, ready to tell the world to go to hell if it didn't like the way he did things.

He thought he had met all of them, but he was mistaken. Going up to his room less than an hour later, he started to take his gun apart to clean it. He had it apart and on the table near the bed when he heard the light knock on the door. Frowning, he stepped to his warbag, slipped out another Colt and placed it on the table next to the one he was cleaning.

When he opened the door a girl was standing there, hatless, her brown hair short and curly. She looked at him, a faint smile playing around the corners of her hazel eyes. She was somewhat taller than Charity McSween, and possibly a few years older. She was wearing a black riding skirt, boots and a white silk blouse.

The door of one of the rooms diagonally across the corridor from Mulvane's was slightly ajar, convincing

Mulvane that the girl had stepped out of her room across to his.

The girl in the doorway said, "You're Mulvane?"

Mulvane nodded.

"I'm Rosslyn Elder," the brown-haired girl said. "You took your damned time getting here, Mulvane. May I come in?"

Mulvane looked at her. "Come in," he said. He'd never seen her before in his life.

Rosslyn Elder strode into the room, closing the door behind her. There was only one chair in the room, and Mulvane had been sitting on it, working on the gun. He pushed the chair toward the girl now and said, "Make yourself at home."

"You're almost two weeks late," Rosslyn Elder said. "What happened?"

Mulvane sat down on the edge of the bed, a faint smile on his face. He said, "Late for what?"

"Maybe you weren't too enthused about the price," Miss Elder said softly. "Is that why you're late?"

Mulvane shrugged. This girl had his name right, but she undoubtedly had the wrong man. Grinning slightly, he thought he'd play out the string a little longer, just for the hell of it. He said, "Maybe I didn't like the price, ma'am."

Rosslyn Elder looked at him steadily for several long moments, and her eyes moved to the gun on the table and then back to him again. "They tell me you're the toughest gunslinger in the Cherokee Strip," she said.

Mulvane shrugged, the humor still in his gray eyes. He'd been in many places, but the Cherokee Strip, hangout for outlaws and loose riders, was unfamiliar country to him.

"I offered you five hundred dollars to make Pleasant Valley safe for my stock," Miss Elder said. "What's your offer now?"

"What's *your* offer now?" Mulvane countered.

Rosslyn Elder looked at him steadily. "It's still five hundred," she said, "and this."

She stepped over to the bed, bent down and kissed him full on the mouth. She moved back then and said softly, "Is the price all right now?"

Mulvane grinned at her. "It was all right before," he said, "if I'm the man you made this deal with."

The girl stared at him, her mouth tight. "What does that mean?" she asked slowly.

The grin on Mulvane's face broadened. He asked softly, "You sure you got the right man?"

"Mulvane," she said.

He nodded. "Mulvane."

"U. P. Mulvane," Rosslyn Elder added, and now it was his turn to stare.

"U.P.?" he repeated softly. "Ulysses Patrocles Mulvane?"

"You're not U. P. Mulvane?" Rosslyn Elder asked him.

"My brother," Mulvane said. He was positive there could only be one U. P. Mulvane in this part of the country. When the nesters had closed in on his father's range years before, squeezing him out and ultimately causing his death, both boys had lit out on their own. U.P. had been three years older than Mulvane and it had been nearly fourteen years since Mulvane had seen his older brother, although occasionally he'd heard stories of a tough gunslinger who went by the name of U. P. Mulvane and who had been putting fear into the hearts of nesters and land agents everywhere.

Miss Elder said, "If you're not Ulysses Patrocles Mulvane, who are you?"

Mulvane merely smiled.

Then Rosslyn Elder stepped up and slapped him hard across the face.

"That's for deceiving me," she said, but she was not particularly angry. She had simply done something a woman had to do for the sake of her dignity.

"Feel better now?" he asked.

"You're a pair," the girl said. "From what I've heard already in this town, you must be just about as tough as your brother."

"Maybe tougher," Mulvane said thoughtfully, remembering the feel of her lips on his.

"Your brother hasn't arrived," Rosslyn Elder said as she took a turn around the room. "Maybe you could be my man."

Mulvane grinned broadly. Fourth offer! he thought amusedly. He said aloud, "You run stock in this Pleasant Valley?"

The girl nodded. "I'm a cattle raiser."

Mulvane lifted his eyebrows. "You're not in the combine with the others?" he asked.

"They're in a war," Miss Elder told him. "This is a private fight for a valley that belongs to me."

"They trying to bring sheep into it?" Mulvane asked next.

The girl nodded. "I'm paying five hundred dollars," she said, "to you — or to your classically named brother, if he ever gets here — to turn them back and keep them out."

"You fighting McSween?" Mulvane asked.

"Not McSween personally," she explained. "Most of the sheepmen are loosely banded together under McSween's leadership, but McSween is not trying to push any of his own flocks down into my valley."

Mulvane walked over to the table and picked up the gun he'd been cleaning. He held it up to the light and looked into the barrel before speaking. Then he said, "You're the fourth one today who's tried to sign me up."

"You could work with me," Miss Elder observed, "until your brother arrives. There is a good possibility he has changed his plans and will not come here at all."

Mulvane thought about that. He would like to see U.P. again after so many years. He wondered how the years had handled his older brother. Evidently U.P. and he had followed the same path, living by the gun. If he stayed here in Boulder City, there was a good possibility he would run into U.P., and while he was waiting he would be earning his keep.

"What claim do you have to Pleasant Valley?" he asked.

"My grandfather stettled it," Rosslyn Elder told him. "We've run cattle there for thirty-five years."

Mulvane smiled. "Reckon that gives you pretty good right to it. How bad has it been?"

"They've run their flocks into the west end of the valley," the girl explained. "My riders have driven them out, but they've come back, and now apparently they have hired guns with them. A few weeks ago one of my men was shot out of the saddle."

"There are sheep in the valley now?" Mulvane asked.

Miss Elder nodded. "I have four men working with me at Slash E," she said, "and one of them is laid up with a bullet wound. I wired to your brother in Grant City, and I've been expecting him daily."

Mulvane put the gun back on the table. He said, "You don't figure Boyd Harmon could help you? If the ranchers are banded together against these sheepmen, it's strange you're not in with them."

Rosslyn Elder's eyes hardened slightly. "Harmon and the others want to drive all the sheepmen off the mountain," she said. "I'm interested only in clearing Pleasant Valley."

Melvane asked, "You ever figure what would happen if McSween backed up the play of this herder trying to push his flocks down into your valley?"

The girl said steadily, "That's the reason I'm hiring a Mulvane. Maybe the one I'm talking to now isn't the one I need."

Mulvane smiled. "I'll be out at Slash E in the morning," he said. "If my brother turns up later and you want him, I'll ride on — or you might want both of us, and we'll split the price."

Rosslyn nodded. "We'll see if he comes."

34

When she turned toward the door she passed within arm's reach of Mulvane, and he put out his hand and touched her shoulder. She looked at him calmly and steadily, and he said, "Reckon I owe you something, Miss Elder, something you gave to me by mistake when you came in here. Like to pay it back."

Then he stepped up to her and kissed her, taking his time about it. He felt her fingers tighten on his arms.

When he stepped back she looked a little flustered. "I don't hire all my riders on this basis, Mulvane," she said. "Please remember that."

"Keep it in mind," he said, grinning, and opened the door for her.

After she'd gone, he sat down at the table again and reassembled his gun, wondering as he did so if U.P. would really turn up in Boulder City. U.P. was already nearly two weeks late; it was very possible he had changed his plans or even forgotten that he had an assignment out here. U.P. had been like that as a boy — easygoing, indifferent, but a real rough one when he got aroused. Mulvane thought that it would be a little odd, riding side by side with Ulysses Patrocles Mulvane at last.

Riding for Rosslyn Elder could prove quite interesting, too, all things considered. That is, unless Jehu McSween decided to take a hand in the doings in Pleasant Valley.

In the morning Mulvane saddled the claybank and rode out of town. He'd eaten a leisurely breakfast and had paused at the clerk's desk in the lobby to ask if Miss

Elder was still in the hotel. He'd been informed that she'd ridden out an hour before. It appeared that both she and Boyd Harmon reserved rooms at the hotel when they came in to town.

"Two-hour ride up to Slash E," the clerk informed him. "Follow the old stage road north till you cross Cheyenne Creek. Half mile past the creek, you'll see the trace leading west into Pleasant Valley."

Leaving town, Melvane rode by Sheriff Rog Denton, who was just coming in astride a big bay horse. Denton slowed down, nodded to him and said, "Taking my advice and pulling out, Mulvane?"

Mulvane shook his head. "Signed on at Slash E," he said, and saw Denton frown.

"Heard Rosslyn was lining up some toughs," Denton said, scowling. "You might have lived longer, mister, riding for me."

Mulvane smiled. "The pay is a lot higher, and I would say Miss Elder is considerably prettier than you."

"Hell with you, too," Rog Denton growled, and he rode on into town.

An hour and a half later Mulvane crossed the ford of Cheyenne Creek and turned into the trace that led out to Pleasant Valley. It was good range land all the way out, and he could see why Harmon and the others were ready to fight for it, just as McSween and the sheepmen were going to fight for their high meadows.

Mulvane hit the east end of Pleasant Valley after following the trace for two or three miles. The valley was low and at least half a mile wide, and it led deep into the foothills of the Owl Head Range, over which he'd come the previous day.

Nestled up against an almost oblique sandstone wall on the far side of the valley, he saw the Slash E spread. Beyond in the valley, clumps of cattle were grazing. The grass here was, if anything, even better than it had been on the open range north of Boulder.

He rode across a meadow, forded a tiny stream that trickled through Pleasant Valley, and then rode around a pole corral to the ranch house proper. Like most buildings in these hills it was a split-log affair, not as large as Jehu McSween's up the mountain, but larger than the ordinary ranch house and shaded by half a dozen large cottonwoods that had been planted years before.

There was a bunkhouse another twenty-five yards from the ranch house, and the man coming out of the bunkhouse to toss away a panful of dirty dish water stopped to look at him as he dismounted in front of the house and tied the claybank to the tie rack.

Rosslyn Elder came out on the porch, then, her curly brown hair catching the light of the mid-morning sun as she came down the steps.

Mulvane said, "Figured you might have waited for me."

"I'm an early riser," Rosslyn told him, "and I thought you might have changed your mind. The deal still holds?"

Mulvane smiled. "I'm here." He looked down toward the bunkhouse, and he saw that two other men had come out to stare at him. He said to the girl, "Your crew?"

"Three of them," Rosslyn Elder said. "Our fourth man is in town with a bullet hole in his shoulder. You want to meet the men now?"

Mulvane nodded. "As good a time as any."

As they walked down toward the bunkhouse, Mulvane sized up the three Slash E riders. They looked like typical cowpokes, good at handling stock but probably not too anxious to mix with the kind of men Jehu McSween was bringing into the country.

Rosslyn Elder said, "Boys, this is Mulvane. He'll be riding with us."

"Give it to them straight," Mulvane said without looking at her. "I'll be giving the orders. That the way you want it, Miss Elder?" He looked at her then and saw her bite her lips.

"All right," she said grimly, "that's the way I want it."

She introduced the three men to Mulvane. Two of them were short, rather stumpy men, and the third man was taller and lean, with a wolfish look about him. The tall man went by the name of Red Bannion, and he had the brightest red hair Mulvane had ever seen.

The shorter men were named Shorty McCabe and Dave Shaw. McCabe was going to fat, and Shaw was a little fellow with bow legs. Mulvane said to them, "You the boys being pushed around by a bunch of damned sheepherders?"

Red Bannion had a cigarette stub in his mouth. He flicked it away now and said caustically, "We'll see how tough you are, mister."

38

Mulvane smiled. "Where are the sheep in this valley?" he asked, looking toward the west.

Rosslyn Elder answered the question. "There has been a big flock at the west end of the valley since Mart Halloran was shot."

"Gunsharps are holed in up there," Shorty McCabe growled. "We go ridin' down there an' we'll get what Mart got — to hell with that."

"How many?" Mulvane asked.

McCabe shrugged. "Last time we went down there," he said, "they opened fire on us when we tried to push their damned sheep up into the hills. Couldn't say how many guns. Maybe four or five. How many you figure, Red?"

"Plenty," Bannion said. "How do you aim to get 'em out o' there, Mulvane?"

"Saddle up," Mulvane said, and he saw Shorty McCabe's jaw sag. The other short man grinned a little — this one he liked.

"Now?" McCabe asked.

"Now," Mulvane told him. "How far away is this flock?"

"Six or seven miles," McCabe said.

Mulvane nodded. "We'll eat first." He looked at Rosslyn Elder as the three men turned back into the bunkhouse. He said, "I eat with the boys?"

She frowned at him. "All my riders eat in the bunkhouse," she snapped.

Mulvane grinned. "Any way you want it, ma'am," he said, and turned toward the bunkhouse. Rosslyn Elder strode away, an angry swing to her hips.

CHAPTER
FIVE

McCabe had evidently been acting as cook, too, and he had beans, sowbelly and sourdough biscuits ready for them. The four men ate silently, no one speaking until they were nearly finished.

Then Dave Shaw asked, "How do you figure on pushin' 'em out, Mulvane?"

"See where they are first," Mulvane told him. "I'm not riding you three boys right into their guns."

Shaw grinned. "Didn't figure you were."

Bannion said, "One thing pushin' 'em out, mister, another thing keepin' 'em out."

"How many sheepmen up in those mountains?" Mulvane asked.

Bannion shrugged. "Must be ten or a dozen," he said. "McSween's the big one."

Mulvane pushed his tin coffee cup away. "Let's ride," he said.

The four men rode away from the ranch and headed west along the south edge of the valley. When they were out of sight of the ranch house, Mulvane turned the claybank in among the trees, leaving the valley and climbing a slight grade.

They rode for another fifteen minutes through the trees, and then Mulvane called a halt. McCabe said, "Reckon you ain't lettin' 'em know we're comin' up, Mulvane. That why we left the valley?"

"I don't ride into a gun," Cass said. "You boys sit it out here now. I'll have a look up ahead. You hear any gunfire, come riding — and come fast."

He moved on as the three others dismounted, and as he left them he caught the odor of sheep. Rosslyn Elder had told him that these sheep had been brought in by a sheep raiser by the name of John Ames. She knew that one herder would be with the flock, but no one seemed to know how many gunhands would be close by.

Circling back toward the valley, Mulvane caught sight of the sheep spread out across the valley floor. It was a large flock, at least six or eight hundred.

He dismounted among the trees and rolled a cigarette, smoked it halfway through and then rubbed it out on a tree trunk before moving forward on foot. The herder would have his wagon parked somewhere close at hand, and he would have a dog, who very soon now would be catching Mulvane's scent, unless the animal was on the far side of the valley with the sheep.

Down close to the valley floor, the trees started to thin out, and Mulvane spotted the sheepherder's round-topped wagon parked in the shade of some cottonwoods. Smoke curled up from a cook fire close at hand.

Mulvane spotted the herder himself a few moments later, as he came up from the stream carrying a pail of water. He saw the dog, too, far across the valley floor. There were no other men in sight.

The herder set the water pail down near the fire, his back toward the spot where Mulvane was still concealed. The herder was evidently in the process of cooking his noonday meal. A coffeepot hung over the fire, and a frying pan rested on a flat rock nearby.

The gunhands Ames had hired to protect his sheep at this end of the valley must have been concealed somewhere close by. Then Mulvane spotted two men riding across the valley, heading toward the herder's wagon. They were only a quarter of a mile away, and Mulvane knew that he had to act immediately.

Tying the claybank among the trees, he walked down the grade toward the sheepherder, who was bent over the fire. As he walked he circled so that the wagon was between himself and the two approaching riders, making it impossible for them to see him.

Coming up close behind the herder, a tall, lean, bearded fellow, Mulvane slipped the gun from the holster and said easily, "Just stand up straight, mister, and then start walking toward that wagon. You make a sound and you're dead."

The herder stiffened as he crouched by the fire, and then his head turned toward the rifle that stood against a box a few yards away.

"You'd be dead before you could reach it," Mulvane informed him. "So don't try. Now stand up, mister."

The herder stood up, his back still toward Mulvane.

"Walk toward the wagon," Mulvane told him. "I'm right behind you."

The herder grumbled something in his throat, but he started to walk when Mulvane stepped up behind him and jammed the gun into the small of his back.

When they reached the wagon, Mulvane said, "You just stay here, mister. I'll be inside. Don't make a sound when your friends come up. I'll have a gun on you all the time."

He stepped in to the rear of the wagon, then, the gun still in his hand, and ordered the herder to back up closer to him.

"Who the hell are you?" the herder growled over his shoulder.

"Keep your mouth shut," Mulvane told him. "If you don't ask too many questions, you might be able to roll this rig out of here without having a bullet hole in you."

The herder said no more, and the two of them waited for the riders to come up. Mulvane said to the man, "Any more beside these two?"

"Go find out," the herder snapped peevishly, and Mulvane leaned forward and cracked him across the hat with the barrel of the six-gun. The herder staggered and nearly fell.

When he'd righted himself and was shaking his head, Mulvane said to him gently, "You remember how many there are, mister?"

"Three," the herder mumbled, and he took off his hat to rub his head vigorously.

"They all come in to eat now?" Mulvane asked him. His question was answered as he spotted a third rider angling across the valley, coming around the flock of sheep.

The two men he'd seen first were now close at hand, and he could hear the clump of their horses' hoofs as they approached the wagon.

"Just relax," Mulvane said softly. "Keep your mouth shut, and you might still be alive by tonight."

The two riders had dismounted near the wagon, and one of them called sharply, "Jake — Jake Garfoyle! Where in hell are you?"

"All right," the herder grumbled.

Mulvane crouched behind him, kneeling on the floor of the wagon, the gun against the herder's back. As the two riders came in sight, Mulvane raised the gun and said, "You boys are covered. The first one goes for his gun is dead."

The two men had been heading toward the fire, but they stopped and stared now, seeing Mulvane in the wagon and looking into the muzzle of his gun.

"Unbuckle the gunbelts," Mulvane said, "and let them drop. You boys are pretty close, and I can't miss. You'll have to hit Jake here before you hit me."

The two riders were typical gunslingers — men of about Mulvane's age, hard-faced, wolfish men. They eyed him speculatively as he crouched behind Jake Garfoyle.

Then one of the men grinned crookedly and said, "Hell with this." He unbuckled his gunbelt and let it fall.

The second man followed him, and then Mulvane said, "Back up toward that fire and sit down. That goes for you, too, Jake — and don't get too near that rifle."

44

The three men moved back toward the fire and sat down. One of the gunslingers started to roll a cigarette, and Mulvane saw him look in the direction of the third rider, who was still several hundred yards away.

"Don't warn him," Mulvane said. "Let him ride in here nice and easy."

The gunhand who had been rolling a cigarette waited until the oncoming rider was within fifty yards of the wagon. Then he called out, "Back off, Gig."

The rider immediately jerked his horse around and shot back across the valley. Mulvane moved away from the wagon and walked toward the three men on the ground. He said to the man who'd given the warning, "Reckon I could have put a bullet through you, mister."

The gunslinger grinned. "Didn't figure you would."

Mulvane smiled grimly. "Ever see a wild mustang creased?" he asked. "Used to do it once in a while when I was chasing the wild ones. You get them across the top of the neck, and you stun them. Doesn't always work because your lead goes a little lower than you figured it would."

The man with the cigarette, a hatchet-faced fellow with a thin nose, looked at him.

"Never tried it with a pistol," Mulvane said. "Rifle's more accurate, but we're closer up here."

He raised his six-gun then and fired, and the lead moved the hat on the hatchet-faced man's head.

"Little too high," Mulvane said, noticing sweat begin to trickle down the gunslinger's face.

"All right," the man mumbled. "All right."

Mulvane said, "Next time, mister, think twice before opening that big mouth of yours. You'll know me next time."

He'd fired the shot mainly to bring on the three Slash E riders, and he sat down on a rock nearby, waiting for them to come up. They came out of the trees a few minutes later, and little Dave Shaw grinned broadly when he saw the three men sitting on the ground.

"Reckon you caught yourself some fish, Mulvane," Shaw said, chuckling.

Mulvane picked up the two gunbelts. He said to the men on the ground, "You boys can pick these up at the sheriff's office in Boulder City on your way out of this country."

"Who says we're goin'?" the second man growled. He was shorter than the first man, and he wore a blond mustache.

"You're leaving," Mulvane said, "or you're dead the next time I see you. Stay out of Pleasant Valley, and get to hell out of this part of the country altogether."

Bannion said, "There were more than this."

"One of them was scared off," Mulvane told him. He said to the man with the mustache, "You tell Gig that goes for him, too. He's dead the next time he sets foot in this valley."

Garfoyle, the sheepherder, said sourly, "You boys talk mighty rough. Maybe you won't be so rough when McSween gets through with you."

Mulvane smiled. "McSween never said he'd back your play in Pleasant Valley. You're throwing a wide loop, Jake, but you're missing the mark."

Garfoyle scowled. "You boys are runnin' into trouble any way you look at it."

"No trouble we can't handle," Mulvane said. "Now get out there with your dog and get those damned sheep moving. I want them out of the valley in an hour, and I don't want them back. You tell your boss that."

To the two gunhands, he said, "Get on your horses and ride out. You're through."

The two men got up from the ground, taking their time. Then they stepped into the saddle and rode west, out of the valley. Garfoyle whistled to his dog and moved off.

Mulvane called after him, "Ames might try to get a sheepherder to move sheep into this valley, Jake. Make damned sure it's not you."

The herder just turned his head and glared back. After he'd gotten the sheep moving, he came back to the wagon to load up and pull out after his flock.

As the four Slash E men rode away, Dave Shaw said curiously, "You figure you can make it stick, Mulvane?"

"My job," Mulvane told him.

Shorty McCabe said, "How in hell you ever get the drop on them two hombres?"

Mulvane looked straight ahead as he rode the claybank. "I sang them a song," he said, his face sober.

As they rode up to Slash E an hour later, Mulvane spotted a dapple gray horse at the tie rack, and Shorty McCabe said, "That'll be Boyd Harmon payin' Miss Elder a visit."

Mulvane looked at the horse as he went by. "Harmon come out here often?" he asked.

"Reckon he gets around," McCabe told him. "He's been friendly enough with Miss Elder."

"Not friendly enough to push those damned woolies out of the valley for her."

McCabe shook his head. "Woman's mind is a curious thing," he said. "The way I look at it, Miss Elder wants to handle this thing herself. I figure by her doin' it this way she keeps McSween out of it. If she'd brought Harmon in, McSween would have had to side with Ames."

Mulvane nodded. It made sense. Rosslyn Elder was no man's fool.

As they rode past the corral they saw Harmon and Rosslyn Elder standing out on the porch. They came out to the edge of the porch as Mulvane and the Slash E men moved past.

"I heard a shot," Rosslyn said. "You run into any trouble?"

Mulvane shook his head. "Sheep are on the way out," he said.

McCabe grinned. "He put the fear into them toughs."

Harmon was standing with his hands hooked in his gunbelt. He said flatly now, "You wouldn't sign up with me, Mulvane, but you signed with Miss Elder, and you're doing the same kind of work I would have had you do."

Mulvane smiled. "What about it?" he asked.

"Any reason why you wouldn't sign up with the cattlemen?" Harmon asked him grimly.

48

"Maybe I don't like cattlemen," Mulvane told him. "I like cattlewomen."

He saw the faint grin that came to Rosslyn Elder's face as he started to ride on again, and noticed that Harmon was glaring after him.

Dave Shaw said as they dismounted near the stable, "Reckon Boyd Harmon would just as soon see you in hell, Mulvane."

"That could be," Mulvane agreed.

After unsaddling the claybank, he sat out in front of the bunkhouse, his chair tilted against the wall of the building, facing the porch where Miss Elder and Boyd Harmon were talking.

Later, Harmon rode off, and the girl walked down toward the bunkhouse. She sat down on the step a few feet from Mulvane and said, "You think they'll try to run sheep back into the valley again?"

"If they do," Mulvane told her, "somebody will find himself dead. They've been warned."

Rosslyn nodded and smiled. "I hired the right man."

Mulvane puffed on his cigarette. "You don't figure you'd do better by throwing in with the ranchers?" he asked. "There it's all for one and one for all."

Rosslyn Elder shook her head. "If the ranchers lose, Pleasant Valley goes first to the sheepmen because part of it is up in the hills. That's the reason I'm fighting my own war."

"It might be a war, too," Mulvane said quietly, thinking of McSween. "It might be a lot bigger war than you figured on."

"Not if McSween's out of it."

"Suppose they get him in?"

Rosslyn frowned. "Aren't you as big as McSween," she asked, "and as tough?"

Mulvane looked at her, wondering if this girl was trying to get him killed.

"We'll see," he said, and let it ride that way.

CHAPTER
SIX

In the morning Mulvane rode in to Boulder City, leaving the two Ames' riders' gunbelts in Rog Denton's office. The sheriff looked at the belts on his battered oak desk and said casually, "Reckon you've already rounded up some culls, Mulvane."

"They rode for a man named John Ames," Mulvane explained. "They were trying to push a flock of sheep down into Pleasant Valley, where they don't belong."

Denton looked at him steadily. "They don't belong — according to Rosslyn Elder," he said. "According to Ames, that might be free range land in the west end of the valley. Miss Elder has never used it. Ames wants to move in there now, and Rosslyn claims the whole damn valley is hers. Who the hell am I supposed to believe?"

Mulvane smiled. "I work for Slash E," he said. "That's who I believe, Sheriff."

Denton scowled. "Easy for you. I'm supposed to look at both sides, mister. Now what in hell are these guns for?"

"Reckon the Ames riders decided they didn't like this part of the country. Turned over their guns to me for safekeeping until they rode out."

"I believe that," Denton told him, "and I'll believe that hell can freeze over."

Crossing the walk to the tie rack where he'd left the claybank, Mulvane heard a man call to him from a saloon door nearby. He stopped and waited, and then he saw Fogarty, the floorman at the Cattleman's Bar, coming out. Fogarty was wearing his brown derby hat and his too-small black suit, and he frowned as he approached.

The floorman said peevishly, "You hit me a hard crack on top of the head, Mr. Mulvane."

Mulvane nodded. "I did that," he agreed.

John Fogarty rubbed his big hands together, cracking the knuckles, and he said, "You wouldn't like to step into an alley now, Mr. Mulvane, and try it again?"

Mulvane shook his head and grinned. "I might not have a bottle in my hand the next time, and I wouldn't take that chance with you, Fogarty. You're too good a man."

Fogarty thought about that. "I can whip you in a fair fight," he said.

Mulvane nodded. "You can whip me," he agreed, "and I'll buy you a drink on that, John." He looked toward the saloon across the street, but Fogarty shook his head, almost in horror.

"Sheep saloon," he said. "Step in here with me, Mr. Mulvane."

They entered the High Dollar Saloon, and Mulvane ordered two drinks at the bar. He said to Fogarty curiously, "You work in the Cattleman's Bar and do your drinking in the High Dollar in the daytime?"

Fogarty chuckled. "I move around. Best beer in town in the High Dollar."

Mulvane nodded. "I'll remember that. They gave me a pretty rough time at the Cattleman the other night."

"Figured you were a McSween man," Fogarty told him. He lifted his glass and said, "Here's to you, Mr. Mulvane. Second best damned fighter in this town."

"Second best," Mulvane agreed, "with fists."

They downed their drinks, and Mulvane clapped the big fellow on the shoulder and walked out of the saloon.

Leaving Boulder City Mulvane turned the claybank into the hills in the direction of the McSween place. He'd decided that morning, at breakfast at the bunkhouse, that he would see Jehu McSween and find out just where he stood as far as Pleasant Valley was concerned.

He wondered how the big sheep raiser was going to take the news that the man he'd tried to hire had signed up with one of the cattle raisers. Working for Rosslyn Elder was not the same as being a gunhand for the cattleman's combine. He wondered, though, if McSween would look upon it in that light.

As he rode out of Boulder that morning, he knew that people were watching him. He'd made a big splash in the town already, and his driving the gunslingers out of Pleasant Valley would not have diminished his reputation.

As he moved up into the hills, he wondered, too, if he would run across the flaxen-haired McSween girl, who had looked at him with interest in her blue eyes.

He passed several flocks of sheep feeding in the meadows, and once a man with a rifle came out to the edge of a clearing to watch him as he crossed a meadow. Mulvane lifted a hand in greeting and kept going.

The man with the rifle watched him suspiciously but made no attempt to stop him. Mulvane was conscious of the fact that he was being watched as he rode through the hills, and he wondered idly how many guns McSween had on his payroll.

He came to the McSween house and was not too much surprised to find Jehu McSween waiting for him, obviously expecting him. McSween sat on the top step of his porch, cradling a lamb gently in his huge arms.

Mulvane sat in the saddle, looking over at the big sheepman.

"You rode way the hell up here from Boulder City," McSween boomed. "You might just as well sit a while, mister."

Mulvane nodded. He tied the claybank to the tie rack and came over to the porch. He sat down on one of the steps and rolled a cigarette.

"Hear you've been raising a little hell down there in Pleasant Valley," McSween said.

Mulvane nodded. "Damn sheepman," he said. "Trying to push sheep into a valley doesn't belong to him."

McSween said caustically, "You've been here two days, mister, and now you're deciding which valleys belong to who. That the way it goes?"

Mulvane turned and smiled up at him. "Everybody in this country tells me Miss Elder has been running stock in that valley for a hell of a long time, and any sheepman tries to bust in there is asking for trouble."

"And any damned cattleman who tries to come up here and push my sheep out of these high valleys is getting himself shot full of lead. You hear that, Mulvane?"

Mulvane nodded. "I don't ride for the cattlemen," he pointed out. "I ride for only one of them, and she's staying where she is."

Jehu McSween laughed through his black beard as he rubbed the neck of the lamb in his lap. "Heard that kind of damned talk before," he said bitterly. "The next thing you know our sheep are pushed higher into the mountains, and the cattlemen have another nice valley for grazing. They've gone as far as we'll let them, now. If that bunch down below tries to take over another foot of grazing land in these hills there'll be hell to pay. You tell Miss Elder that, too, mister.

"And now," McSween went on quietly, "I'd like to know what the hell brings you up into these hills. Any one of my boys could have put a bullet through you on the way up. Reckon you know that."

Mulvane nodded. "Figured I'd like to know where you stood in Pleasant Valley," he said. "You backing Ames' play there?"

McSween looked at him steadily. "John Ames is a damned fool if he's moving sheep down into that valley. He didn't figure on running into anybody as tough as you are."

Mulvane puffed on his cigarette. "That's what I wanted to know," he said.

"You got a fight with Ames," McSween told him, "it's your fight. You try to move beef up the mountain, mister, and that's my fight. And I'm making it a hell of a fight, too."

"You'll be in a bigger one," Mulvane told him coolly, "if you or any other damned sheep raiser tries to move sheep down into Pleasant Valley. Slash E is my brand now. I'm paid to keep you out."

"Reckon we understand each other." McSween smiled coldly.

Mulvane stood up and walked toward the claybank, and as he did so he caught a glimpse of Charity McSween running down the trace, up which he'd come a short while before. She was keeping herself concealed among the trees, and she'd left the house by a rear door so he wouldn't see her.

Mulvane rode off, then, leaving McSween watching him from the porch, and went back down the trail. He rode slowly, expecting to meet the McSween girl down below. He was not particularly surprised when she stepped out from among the trees to confront him.

Pulling up the claybank, he sat there looking down at her, and then he said, "Reckon you wanted to see me, Miss McSween."

"I wanted to warn you," the girl told him quietly. "I think you were a fool to come up into these hills in the first place."

"Was I?"

56

Charity scowled. "You've made two bad enemies to begin with in Beemish and Tolivar, and they're setting you up down along this trail."

Mulvane dismounted. "I'm obliged to you, ma'am," he said. Then he looked down into her blue eyes, the bluest he had ever seen, and added, "How do you know?"

"I saw Beemish and Tolivar back by the horse sheds," Charity explained. "When they saw you ride in, they saddled up immediately and walked their horses off among the trees so you wouldn't see them. I'm positive they've circled to meet you as you come down the trace."

Mulvane smiled. "You don't want to see me shot up?"

Charity looked away. "Why should I?" she countered.

"I work for the cattlemen now," Mulvane said. "Or at least a cattlewoman. I suppose you've heard that."

"I've heard it," Charity said, a slight frown on her face. "Do you enjoy working for a woman?"

Mulvane shrugged and smiled. "Pay is high."

"You could have gotten high pay from Boyd Harmon or from my father."

"I don't like sheep," Mulvane said, "and I didn't like Harmon. That leaves only Miss Elder."

"You're welcome to her," Charity told him, and she turned to go.

Mulvane put a hand on her arm and said, "I'm obliged to you, Charity McSween, for coming here."

The girl stopped and looked up at him, as though she knew what he intended to do but was undecided whether she should move on or wait. Mulvane gave her little time to consider. He bent his head and kissed her, and then, as he tried to put his arms around her, she pushed away from him hard, using her hands as levers against his chest.

"Maybe you can do that to Miss Elder," she said, "but not to me."

Mulvane laughed. "I had to find out, and I reckon I was wrong. I've been wrong before."

"You were wrong," Charity snapped, her face flushed now. "Now go on down that trail and hope you don't get a bullet in your back."

She walked off through the trees then, heading back up toward the house. Mulvane stepped into the saddle again. Beemish and Tolivar were as dangerous as snakes, and they would be fighting as snakes now, striking from ambush. If they had been set up down below along this trace, somebody was going to die.

After leaving Charity McSween, he rode another hundred yards or so down the trail and then turned off in among the trees. Fifty yards off the trace, he tied the claybank in a pine grove. Then he stretched out on the warm pine needles, pulled his hat over his eyes and slept for nearly half an hour.

He awoke and smoked a cigarette, then moved back toward the trace on foot, located a deadfall close by the trace and crawled in among the broken, twisted trees.

Drawing his gun, he placed it on a root outcropping nearby, within arm's reach, and then he made himself as comfortable as possible down in the hole created by the uprooted trees.

58

He waited.

The afternoon was warm up in the hills, and some of the sun's rays penetrated down into the deadfall as Mulvane fitted his lean, rangy body against the trunk of a tree. As he lay there, a squirrel came out, chattered at him and then moved on again. Off in the distance he could hear the bleating of sheep and the distant bark of a dog. Farther back up the trace, at the McSween house, someone was chopping wood, the sound reaching Mulvane very faintly through the woods.

He must have been lying in the deadfall for nearly twenty minutes when he heard the first sounds down along the trace. He sat up, then, reaching for the gun, and peered out between the tree trunks. In a few minutes he spotted two riders coming up the trace, and he immediately recognized Beemish's blue roan and Tolivar's buckskin. The two men would pass within ten yards of where Mulvane was crouching. He let them come on.

He sat up now, cocking the hammer of the gun, and waited until they came abreast of the deadfall. Reese Beemish was riding a little ahead of Tolivar, his hat pushed back on his sandy head and a look of disgust in his tough, pale blue eyes.

Mulvane could hear Tolivar say, "Reckon he ain't stayin' this long up at old McSween's. You figure he could o' gone down the mountain some other way?"

Beemish scowled. "Ain't no damned reason. Why should a man break trail down this mountain when there's a trace here to follow?"

"Reason enough," Tolivar growled, "if he figured somebody was layin' for him down below."

Mulvane called softly from the deadfall, "Reckon somebody *was* waiting for me below, boys."

Both men pulled their horses to a stop, and Beemish jerked out his gun, firing as soon as the muzzle cleared the holster.

Beemish's horse moved as Mulvane fired, and his lead missed the tall man and caught Tolivar full in the chest.

Little Tolivar crumpled, his arms cringing across his chest, and then he fell forward from the saddle, his body hitting the ground like a sack of wheat.

Reese Beemish dug his spurs into the flanks of the roan horse, and the animal shot down the trace and out of sight among the trees. Mulvane climbed out of the deadfall, gun in hand, and walked up to the trace. The buckskin horse Tolivar had been riding had started up the trail toward the McSween place.

Bending down, Mulvane rolled the small man over, looked at him and then straightened up. Ed Toliver was as dead as any man would ever be. The bullet had caught him just above the breastbone, and there was an expression of complete surprise on his small, squinting face.

Mulvane could still hear Beemish rocketing down the side of the mountain, and he didn't think it worth while to give chase now. Beemish had too big a start. But Mulvane knew one thing — the next time he ran across Beemish, he was going to kill him.

Walking back to where he'd left the claybank, Mulvane mounted and rode back up toward the McSween house. He was positive they had heard the shots down the trace and would be wondering what had happened.

When he'd gone a short way, he saw Tolivar's buckskin feeding in a small meadow to the right of the trace. He caught up with the horse and led it back up the hill to the house.

Jehu McSween had come from the house, and was looking down the grade as Mulvane came up leading Tolivar's horse. Charity McSween stood on the porch, and Mulvane wondered if she had been concerned after hearing the shots.

Nearing McSween, Mulvane slapped the buckskin on the rump. The horse trotted on toward the sheds beyond the house.

McSween said flatly, "Shooting down below, and that's Tolivar's horse."

"Tolivar and Beemish tried to set me up down below along the trace."

"Bushwhack job," McSween scowled. "Had it in mind to fire those two bums anyway. So Tolivar's dead?"

Mulvane nodded.

"And Beemish will be when you catch up with him," McSween added. "That it?"

"That's it," Mulvane said.

"Still don't want to ride for me?" McSween asked softly.

Mulvane smiled down at him. "When you start raising beef, Mr. McSween," he said, and he turned the claybank and started down the trace again.

CHAPTER
SEVEN

It was nearly dusk when Mulvane rode back in to Boulder City. Rather than riding on to Slash E, he decided to have his supper in town, and he turned in again at the same restaurant he'd eaten in his first night here.

He was dismounting at the tie rack in front of the restaurant when he saw Griff Bannerman, Boyd Harmon's ramrod, angling across the street toward him. Bannerman had seen him ride in, and was coming over now to talk.

Mulvane waited for him on the walk. There was something about Bannerman that he didn't like. His smile was too genial; he had been too friendly that first time they'd met on the porch in front of the Cattleman's Bar. This was a man who could smile and smile and smile — and then stick a knife in your back.

Bannerman grinned as he came up on the walk. "Hear you gave some of those damned sheep riders a little hell up in Pleasant Valley, Mulvane."

"We pushed them out," Mulvane told him briefly. "What is it you want, Bannerman?"

Bannerman smiled. "Saw you headin' over here. Figured I'd like a cup of coffee myself. Had my supper a while back."

Mulvane said, "Ranch men in these parts spend more time in the damned town than they do out on the range."

"Might be more doing in town," Bannerman said with a chuckle. "Buy you a drink after you've had your supper?"

Mulvane shrugged and turned to go into the restaurant and Bannerman came along behind him. Mulvane sat at a table, and as he was ordering his meal Bannerman came from the counter carrying a cup of hot coffee. He set it down on the table across from Mulvane, kicked back a chair and said, "Might be a little excitement in this town tonight, Mulvane. Figured you'd like to know."

Mulvane looked at him. "Why would I want to know?" he asked.

Bannerman stirred his coffee with a spoon. "You might like to know that a few of our boys worked over one of McSween's herders today. Soon as he gets word of it, I wouldn't be a damned bit surprised if he came riding in here, looking for the men who did it."

Mulvane sat back in his chair. He said, "Denton wants to keep this fight out of the town. Why do you bring it in here?"

Bannerman lifted his short-fingered hands helplessly, the smile still on his face. "McSween's fight," he pointed out. "Our boys kicked his herder and sheep to hell out of one of the upper valleys, which happens to be Circle H range. This being Saturday night, a lot of the boys will be in town, and McSween will know that."

"You could stop a fight," Mulvane observed, "by ordering your boys to ride out."

Bannerman looked at him. "You figure they'd ride?" he asked gently. "These boys were hired for trouble, Mulvane, and they don't run."

"So shoot the hell out of yourselves." Mulvane smiled evenly, and then he saw Rog Denton coming into the restaurant and moving toward an empty table.

When Denton spotted him across the room, he slowed up. Mulvane hooked a finger at him, inviting the lawman to join them. Denton sat down at the table, tossing his hat onto a peg nearby.

He said to Bannerman, his voice tight, "Hear some of your boys had a run-in with a McSween herder back up in the hills this afternoon."

Bannerman nodded. "You heard right. McSween's trying to push his woolies down the mountain."

"And maybe you're pushing your beef up the mountain," Denton told him thinly. "Damned if I've ever heard before that Boyd Harmon was grazing his stock that far up the ridge."

Bannerman shrugged. "Our range," he said. "Reckon we can graze our stock any damned place we please, Rog."

Mulvane said to Denton, "Bannerman here figures McSween and some of his crew might ride in here tonight to look up the boys who jumped his herder. You might like to know about that."

Denton stared at Bannerman, the dislike plain in his faded gray eyes. "You itching to have somebody killed, Griff?" he asked.

The Circle H ramrod again held up his hands helplessly. "My boys are on their own now, Rog," he said. "If McSween rides in here looking for trouble, what in hell can I do about it?"

Rog Denton looked at him and said no more.

When Bannerman had finished his coffee and left, Mulvane said to the sheriff, "You figure McSween will come in tonight?"

Rog Denton shook his head and scowled. "I don't figure Jehu will take this sitting down," he said. "If he takes this, he'll have to take more. Reckon he knows."

Mulvane nodded. "You aim to stop him?"

"Can't stop a man from riding in here," Denton said glumly, "nor from throwing lead if somebody else draws on him."

Mulvane grinned. "You should have more deputies, Denton," he said.

Rog Denton looked at him distastefully. "Pay wasn't high enough for you, was it?"

Mulvane sipped his coffee. "Not only the pay," he said. "The odds weren't good, either, Denton, and I always play the odds."

As Mulvane stepped out of the restaurant, leaving Denton to finish his supper, he saw little Dave Shaw from Slash E going by on the walk, headed for the nearest saloon, licking his lips in anticipation. Evidently he had just ridden in.

Shaw pulled up. "Where the hell you been, Mulvane?" he asked. "Miss Elder is wonderin' about you."

"She can wonder," Mulvane said. "There are no sheep in Pleasant Valley, are there?"

Shaw grinned. "No sheep."

"She didn't hire me to play nursemaid to cows."

Shaw had some other information. "John Ames, the sheepman, is in town," he said. "Went in to the Owl Head Bar."

"I might have a drink," Mulvane said, and he moved across the road in the direction of the Owl Head. As he was crossing the street he noticed that little Shaw was coming up behind him.

Shaw laughed. "Reckon I got a dry on, too. I'll buy you one, Mulvane."

Mulvane smiled at him. "Might be a lot safer buying your drinks in the Cattleman's Bar."

"Hell with that," Shaw said. "If you go in, guess I can go in, mister."

Mulvane shrugged. They pushed in through the bat-wing doors together, finding the Owl Head Saloon considerably smaller than the Cattleman's Bar, but fairly crowded. The sheepmen and local nester who came in here for their drinks were a different breed from the men Mulvane had seen in the Cattleman's Bar. These were men of the soil, most of whom walked on foot and many of whom were not even armed. But there were a few others — hard-bitten men with guns in their holsters — who were evidently loose riders for the sheepmen.

Dave Shaw said, "Ames is the tall fellow in black at the far end of the bar."

Mulvane saw a tall, fairly slender man in a black suit and expensive black boots drinking alone at the other end of the bar. Mulvane figured him to be about his own age, possibly a few years older.

Ames turned slightly as he drank, and his eyes fell upon Mulvane as Mulvane moved down the bar toward him. Like most of the sheepmen he was unarmed, and Mulvane wondered idly whether this was because he didn't use a gun or because it was safer.

Moving up to him, Mulvane said, "Mr. Ames?"

Ames nodded and smiled briefly, revealing a set of very white teeth beneath his carefully trimmed black mustache. His eyes were black and speculative. "I'm John Ames," he said. "What can I do for you?"

"The name's Mulvane," Mulvane said, as he leaned on the bar, half facing the tall man. "I ride for Slash E."

Ames raised his eyebrows slightly, but the smile was still on his face. Mulvane began to realize that Ames was no more an ordinary sheep raiser than was Jehu McSween.

"Hear you had a run-in with some of my riders yesterday," Ames said. "You drove one of my flocks out of the west end of Pleasant Valley."

Mulvane nodded. "Warned your boys off," he said, "and I told your herder not to bring any more sheep into the valley."

"That what you came to tell me, too?" Ames asked softly.

"Reckon you know it," Mulvane told him. "Pleasant Valley is range land. Miss Elder has been using it for a good many years. She intends to keep stock in the valley."

John Ames had been holding an empty liquor glass in his hand. He put it down now and said, "You've told me, Mr. Mulvane. Is that all?"

Mulvane nodded. "That's it. You like to have a drink on it?"

Ames laughed. "Why not?"

Little Dave Shaw said in a low voice to Mulvane, "First damned time I ever had a sheepman buy a drink for me."

"Get used to it," Mulvane said, smiling. "They may take over the country someday."

Shaw scowled. "Like hell."

As he pushed the bottle toward Mulvane and watched him pour two drinks, John Ames said, "Seems I've heard your name before, Mr. Mulvane."

"Not up this way," Mulvane assured him. "New country for me."

"Like it?" Ames asked.

"The pay's good," Mulvane said.

Ames said. "Supposing I was to go higher than Miss Elder?"

Mulvane lifted the liquor glass to study it, and a wide grin spread over his face. "Had four offers to work in this country," he said. "You're number five, Ames. Reckon I'll ride with the hand I've got, though."

John Ames shrugged. "One thing I'd like to tell you, then, Mr. Mulvane, before you leave."

"What is that?" Mulvane asked him amiably.

"You warned me to keep my sheep out of Pleasant Valley," the sheep raiser said softly, "and now I'm warning you. Keep your beef *in* Pleasant Valley."

Mulvane nodded. "Fair enough," he said. "My job is Pleasant Valley. Obliged for the drink." He walked out of the saloon with Dave Shaw.

Outside, he said to Shaw, "Miss Elder ever try to push beef into those upper meadows, Dave?"

Dave Shaw shook his head. "Been enough grazing room in Pleasant Valley all these years," he said, and then he added thoughtfully, "I will say, though, that Miss Elder did put through an order with Boyd Harmon for three hundred more head of beef. They're to move the stock into the valley sometime next week."

Mulvane thought about that, wondering what Rosslyn Elder had in the back of her mind. He wondered, too, whether John Ames had heard about the extra beeves the girl was bringing into the Valley.

"Any good card games going on in this town?" Mulvane asked the Slash E rider.

"Always a few good games going on in the Cattleman's Bar," Shaw told him, "and I reckon they won't try to throw you out of there tonight. Everybody around here knows you ride for Slash E."

Crossing the road to the Cattleman's Bar, Mulvane saw Rog Denton come out of the restaurant and stand on the walk for a few moments, looking up and down the street. Denton was evidently wondering if and when Jehu McSween would ride into Boulder looking for the Harmon riders who'd worked over his herder.

70

Stepping into the Cattleman's Bar, Mulvane spotted Fogarty, the floorman, near the door. The big ex-pugilist grinned at him and lifted a hand. As Mulvane moved past him, heading for one of the card tables, Fogarty said, "In the right place now, Mr. Mulvane."

Up at the bar, the bartender who'd given him trouble just looked at him sourly, his feelings probably still hurt from the way Mulvane had treated him.

There was an empty seat at one of the tables, and Mulvane paused behind the chair, looking at the men in the game. One of them nodded to him, and he pulled out the chair and sat down.

"Stud," one of the players said, and Mulvane was in the game. As a waiter moved by, Mulvane stopped him to order some chips from the bar. Then he sat back, waiting for the chips to come, and put a cigar in his mouth. He looked around the room and noticed that Boyd Harmon was not around. If McSween was coming into Boulder tonight, Harmon should have been here to back up his men.

Griff Bannerman was at the bar, though, and he nodded to Mulvane at the table, the usual broad smile on his face. As Mulvane was drawing his first cards he saw Stub McCabe coming in through the doors.

McCabe joined little Dave Shaw at the bar, had a quick drink, and then headed for Mulvane's table.

The short rider said with a grin, "Miss Elder don't like that you rode off this mornin', Mulvane."

"Any sheep in the valley?" Mulvane asked him.

"Not a damn one," McCabe admitted.

"Hell with her," Mulvane told him, and he looked at his cards.

McCabe went back to the bar, grinning and shaking his head. He joined Dave Shaw there, and the two men tilted glasses again.

Mulvane played half a dozen hands, winning one fairly good pot, losing others. More and more riders were coming into the Cattleman's Bar. Many of them, he realized, were gunslingers for Harmon and the other ranchers in and around Boulder. He still didn't see Harmon, though, and after a while he noticed that Bannerman had left.

Sheriff Denton came into the bar, looked around, spoke for a few moments with Fogarty near the door, and then went out again. And Mulvane wondered whether the sheriff would ever have any luck in lining up a deputy or two to assist him. He felt a little sorry for Denton, but he told himself that the sheriff was a damned fool to begin with. In a situation like this a smart man would look the other way, and, if the sheepmen and cattlemen were intent on shooting each other up, he should let them do it — and to hell with them.

Less than thirty minutes after Denton had moved on, a man yelled in over the bat-wing doors, "Jehu McSween's in town, and he's got a dozen riders with him!"

CHAPTER
EIGHT

Mulvane sat in his chair in the Cattleman's Bar, noticing how quiet the cattlemen had suddenly become. They knew that McSween was not riding in here with a dozen sheepherders, but with a dozen tough gunslingers who'd been hired to throw lead.

Sitting at the table, facing the bat-wing doors, Mulvane watched McSween ride by a few moments later. McSween was astride a huge black stallion, and he rode with a shotgun across the pommel of the saddle. As he went by he turned his bearded face to look in over the doors, and then he kept riding, a dozen men trailing behind him. Evidently, in his search for the pair who'd jumped his herder, McSween intended to work down from the farthest saloon in town and then come back toward the Cattleman's Bar.

Boyd Harmon was still not in town. Mulvane had not thought that Harmon was the kind of man who would leave his riders out on a limb in a situation like this. There was, of course, the possibility that Harmon, Bannerman and the Circle H riders had gathered some place nearby and were getting ready to confront McSween.

The man out on the walk who'd called into the saloon now said over the doors, "They're lookin' in the Great Western."

One of the men at the card table with Mulvane said to the player at his left, "I've got only three riders in town tonight, Davis. I'm not bucking him. Not with twelve."

Mulvane said, leaning across the table, "Where's Harmon?"

Davis, a short, heavy-set man, shook his head. "Damned if I know," he said.

Mulvane suddenly saw how it was in town tonight. The cattlemen were present, but there was no real organization, no one to line up the different riders from each outfit and put up a concerted front against McSween. These men needed a leader. The leader should have been Boyd Harmon.

A minute or so later Jehu McSween pushed in through the doors of the Cattleman's Bar, coming in as though he were walking into a stable. He was still carrying the shotgun, and he paused just inside the door, the gun across his body. His blue eyes were bleak and tough as he searched the room, towering above the men near him, his heavy legs spread.

His eyes rested for a moment on Mulvane at the table, and Mulvane nodded to him briefly, a smile on his face. A heavy silence had settled over the room when McSween came in. In the back room a man was laughing in a high-pitched, drunken voice, but the laughter stopped abruptly.

74

McSween said tersely, "I'm looking for two dogs who jumped one of my herders up in the hills. They ride for Circle H, and, if they're in this town tonight, they'll be getting a dose of what they gave my man."

His crew were bunched in the door behind him, but Mulvane was positive that McSween would have come in here alone in order to ferret out the Harmon riders.

As McSween looked around the room, Sheriff Rog Denton pushed in through his crew. Denton said quietly, "I don't want any shooting in this town, McSween."

Jehu McSween didn't even look at him. He said, "You have an ordinance in this town against carrying a gun?"

"No ordinance," Denton admitted.

McSween nodded. "You'd be a smart man to keep out of this, Denton. No man alive can ride up into my hills, jump one of my herders and bust him up the way they did and then ride away from it. I'm looking for two boys by the name of Hanlon and O'Neil, and they'd better not try to ride out of this town tonight because I've got half a dozen more men stationed at both ends of Boulder."

No one spoke. Mulvane felt a growing contempt for the absent Bannerman. In Harmon's absence, Bannerman should have stood up for his crew.

McSween walked over to the door opening on the back room and looked in. Then he kicked in another door behind the bar, disappeared for a moment and then came out again.

It was Mulvane's deal, and he shuffled the cards as he watched McSween walk back toward the entrance.

Rog Denton said to the big sheep raiser, "You have any complaints against these two boys, bring a formal charge and I'll pick them up myself."

"Hell with your formal charges," McSween snapped. "Any jury in this town would be hand-picked, and you know how much chance I'd stand in a court of law."

Rog Denton didn't have any answer to this, and McSween brushed by him and went out into the street, followed by his crew. They headed down toward the next saloon.

Instead of dealing his cards, Mulvane dropped the deck on the table and said simply, "I'm out, boys. Reckon I'd like to see the fun." Then he moved to the bar to cash in his chips and walked out, joining the crowd outside the door.

As he emerged from the saloon he saw McSween coming out of the High Dollar and heading up toward the hotel beyond. A small hunch-backed man was trying to push past Mulvane as he stood on the walk with the crowd, and Mulvane obligingly stepped away to let the man go by. As he did so he looked back in the other direction and caught sight of a man running across the road. Mulvane got a brief but clear glimpse of him as he darted across a patch of light from a second-floor window. The man running across the road, carrying a rifle in his hands, was Griff Bannerman.

Thoughtfully, Mulvane stepped back until he was at the edge of the crowd. Then he looked again toward the

76

alley into which Bannerman had run. The Circle H ramrod had been alone. If he had been preparing some kind of ambush for McSween, he would have had other Circle H riders with him.

McSween and his men were moving down the boardwalk toward the hotel. Mulvane looked once more at the alley into which Bannerman had gone, and then, on an impulse, he turned and walked down the street, eventually cutting across the road and entering the same alley.

He was positive Bannerman was now circling up the street, intending to come abreast of McSween and his crew.

Moving up the alley to the far end, Mulvane paused and listened carefully. He could hear someone making his way across back lots, and every once in a while he caught a glimpse of a bulky figure hurrying past a patch of light from a window.

Mulvane followed, keeping back in the shadows against the rear wall of the building. Bannerman passed two alleys and then turned down the third. As he disappeared from sight, Mulvane hurried to catch up with him. Off to his right as he ran, he'd seen a horse tied. The horse, saddled and ready to go, could mean that Bannerman had planned a quick getaway after shooting down McSween or some of his riders.

Skulking in an alley here meant only one thing to Mulvane — Bannerman was in the same class with Beemish and Tolivar. Sliding the gun from his holster, Mulvane edged down into the alley, which opened on the main street again. He could see Bannerman up ahead of him, his blocky figure reflected in the light from the street. The alley opened directly across from the Cheyenne Saloon, into which McSween had just gone. The men with him were grouped outside the door, some of them smoking and looking up and down the street.

Bannerman had stopped now, and Mulvane could see him clearly as he knelt down, raised his rifle and lined it on one of McSween's crew out on the street. Mulvane was still perplexed. If Bannerman wanted to hit at McSween, the best way to do it was to knock down the big sheep raiser himself, and Bannerman had only to wait another few moments until McSween came out of the saloon.

Bannerman was not interested in this, however. He intended only to drop a McSween man, sprint back up the alley to his horse and ride out. He probably did not know of the McSween men guarding both approaches to the town, or possibly he knew and had planned a route out another way.

Lining his gun on Griff Bannerman, Mulvane opened his mouth to call to him. As he did so, he stepped a trifle closer to the wall, farther back into the shadows, so Bannerman would not see him if he swung around suddenly with the rifle.

But before Mulvane could get a word out of his mouth, a gun roared in the alley behind him. He felt the tug of the lead as it grazed his right shoulder, and he realized that he would have been dead had he not moved to his left at exactly the right moment.

78

Leaping across the alley to the far wall, Mulvane threw one quick shot back in the direction of the killer who'd pulled down on him. Then he started to run forward. When he reached the head of the alley he heard someone running off toward his right, the direction from which both he and Bannerman had come.

It was quite evident that, as he had followed Bannerman, another man had followed him, and Mulvane had a pretty good idea who that man was. As he took off after the running killer, he heard Bannerman stumbling up the alley, running toward the horse. McSween's crew would be coming into that alley at any moment to see who had thrown that shot, naturally assuming that the lead had been directed at them. A Circle H man found in the alley opposite the Cheyenne Saloon would most certainly be a dead man in short order unless he got out of there.

Mulvane ran at top speed after the man ahead of him, catching a glimpse of him as he crossed a street. Then he saw him enter the rear door of a building.

Running harder, Mulvane lunged over a low fence, reached the doorway into which his man had gone and broke through. He found himself in a private house with a hallway that ran down to another doorway. There was a light in the hall, and Mulvane entered just in time to see the door at the other end of the hall closing.

The man had entered the rear door and emerged back on the main street. Lunging down the corridor, Mulvane burst out into the street and saw the fellow darting up the alley that led to the Emerald Livery Stable.

As Mulvane sprinted across the road he caught a glimpse of McSween's men scattering and swinging up behind the alley from which the shot had come. McSween was standing out in front of the Cheyenne Saloon booming orders at his men, but Mulvane didn't think any of them had seen him or the man he was pursuing.

The man up ahead sprinted in through the open doors of the stable, and, as he passed under a lantern just inside the door, Mulvane got his first good look at him. The man was Reese Beemish.

Swinging off to his right, Mulvane kept out of the line of fire from the door. As he ran over to the building the lantern was smashed, plunging the stable into darkness. Coming up to the wall of the building, Mulvane grasped the heavy door and gave it a push. The hinges squeaked as the door swung shut, closing Beemish in.

As Mulvane pushed the door shut, a man came out of a nearby building and said to him curiously, "You wantin' a horse, mister?"

"Is there a back door to this place?" Mulvane asked him.

"No back door," said the hostler, a wizened old man with bent shoulders. He grinned. "Who the hell is in there, mister?" he asked.

"A dead man," Mulvane told him. "Stay out of the way, old man." He moved down the right wall of the stable, noting that there were several windows, but all of them quite high up.

There was a ladder lying against the wall. Mulvane remembered seeing an open hay loft just above the door. Picking up the ladder, he moved quietly back to the front of the building with it.

Since he was carrying the long ladder with both hands, he would have been an easy mark for Reese Beemish if Beemish had suddenly kicked open the door and started firing. Beemish, however, not having the nerve to work it that way, was skulking inside in the dark, waiting for Mulvane to come in.

The old man watched as he lifted the ladder and placed it gently against the loft opening. He climbed the ladder swiftly, stepping in onto the pile of hay in the loft. Sinking down into the sweet-smelling hay, gun in hand, he waited until his eyes became accustomed to the darkness.

Mulvane could hear horses stamping restlessly below him, but he could see nothing. After a while, when he could distinguish the outlines of the loft in which he was lying, he made his way carefully across the hay to the edge of the loft, which looked down on the floor of the stable. The faint light that came in through the cobwebbed windows on either side of the stable enabled him to make out the vague outlines of a number of horses in the stalls. At least half of the stalls were empty.

There was an alley running down the center of the stable, with stalls on either side of the lane. Reese

Beemish could be directly below, in one of the stalls facing the door, waiting for Mulvane to make his play.

Moving very slowly, Mulvane leaned his weight over the edge of the loft to look down. A horse snorted nervously at the far end of the stable as though anticipating trouble.

With the gun in his right hand, Mulvane took off his hat, placed it on the hay beside him and then leaned farther down so he could look into the stalls directly beneath him. He still couldn't see Beemish. Mulvane leaned out of the loft — waiting, listening carefully.

Outside, the little hostler was calling sharply, "What in hell's goin' on in there?"

Mulvane lay still, looking down from the loft, waiting for Beemish to make the first move and knowing that he would. Beemish had no idea where Mulvane was; he'd be watching the door.

Someone cursed softly down near the door, and then Mulvane saw where Beemish was concealed. Several bundles of straw were piled in one corner of the stable, near the door on the left side of the building, and Beemish was crouched down behind them.

Mulvane raised his gun. He was about to call out to him when Beemish got up suddenly and moved swiftly down toward the far end of the stable, to look at the windows near the rear.

He came back, and, when he was almost underneath, Mulvane called down softly, "Went the wrong way, Beemish."

Beemish leaped for an empty stall nearby, at the same time throwing his first shot in Mulvane's direction. Mulvane had rolled back on the hay as he spoke, and Beemish's bullet gouged splinters out of the edge of the loft.

Coming up on his stomach, Mulvane fired twice, smashing Beemish back into a corner of the stall. He heard Beemish crying out in pain like a small boy and then heard the man's gun fall to the floor of the stall.

Beemish cursed steadily, futilely, as he died.

Outside the little hostler was calling loudly, "Denton — Rog Denton!"

Mulvane put on his hat, clicked out the empty shells, put two fresh cartridges into the cylinder and then put the gun back into the holster. He located the ladder and climbed down.

When he reached the floor, the stable door opened. The shooting had drawn both Denton and McSween up to the Emerald Livery Stable, and Denton was calling sharply, "Who's in there?"

"Strike a light," Mulvane told him. "Shooting's over."

Someone came in with a lantern, then, and Denton looked at Mulvane curiously as he walked back toward the stall where Beemish was lying. McSween came in, too, followed by some of his riders.

"Who the hell's doing the shooting in here?" McSween demanded. "Plenty of lead flying, and nobody man enough to take it back."

Denton said, "Mulvane's in here."

McSween came in then and stood beside Mulvane, looking down at Reese Beemish as Denton bent over him with a lighted lantern.

"Try to bushwhack you again?" McSween asked.

Mulvane nodded. "This time I caught up with him," he said.

McSween scowled. "Good-by to nothing."

He stood there for a moment, frowning, and Mulvane wondered if he ought to tell the big sheep raiser what Griff Bannerman had been doing in the alley opposite the Cheyenne Saloon. Then he decided to keep the information to himself, for whatever it was worth. Bannerman still didn't know who had been behind him in the alley, and he'd evidently gotten away.

Rog Denton was saying, "You chase him in here, Mulvane?"

Mulvane nodded.

"He had a gun with him," Denton observed, "and he threw some lead at you. I'd guess it was a case of self-defense."

"You guessed damn right," Mulvane said dryly.

"This begin in that alley across from the Cheyenne Saloon?" Denton asked.

Mulvane nodded.

Denton scowled. "None of my business, I suppose, but what in hell were you doing in that alley?"

Mulvane smiled at him. "You said it. None of your business, Sheriff."

"May be my business," McSween said significantly. "My boys were right opposite that alley when that shot was fired."

Mulvane looked at him. "Reckon I'm no bush-whacker, McSween," he said.

McSween nodded and asked, "Somebody else in that alley besides you and Beemish?"

"Why not take a look?" Then Mulvane smiled and walked out of the stable.

CHAPTER
NINE

The crowd had headed down toward the Emerald Stable when they heard the shooting, and now they were trickling back up the street. Dave Shaw fell in step with Mulvane as he walked back toward the Cattleman's Bar.

Mulvane said to the little Slash E rider, "They find those two Harmon men yet?"

"Still lookin'," Shaw said. "You in that shootin'?"

Mulvane nodded. "I was in it."

As they neared the Cattleman's Bar, there was a shout from the other end of town, and then some of McSween's crew came down, herding two men before them.

Shaw said softly, "Reckon they caught up with the Harmon boys, Mulvane."

Mulvane pulled up in front of the Cattleman's Bar, and as he did so McSween strode past him, heading toward the group coming down the street.

"Be hell to pay," Shaw said. "Let's see the fun, Mulvane."

Mulvane followed McSween along the walk as men came running from all directions, forming a circle about the McSween riders and the two Harmon men they'd smoked out.

"You'd figure these cattlemen wouldn't take this," Shaw said.

"Reckon you're taking it," Mulvane observed.

Shaw chuckled. "Hell, I'm not stickin' my neck out for Boyd Harmon tonight. He wants his riders to act tough, he ought to be here to back their play when they get in trouble. Same goes for Griff Bannerman."

Mulvane and Dave Shaw stood on the outskirts of the crowd, watching as McSween confronted the two Harmon riders.

"Bring me a whip," McSween said grimly. "I want these two dogs tied to a tie rack. Strip 'em down."

The McSween men rushed the two unfortunate Harmon riders over to the nearest tie rack, and they tied their hands to the bar while someone handed McSween a bull-whip.

The big sheep raiser strode out to the tie rack, cracking the whip as he did so.

Before he could use it, however, Rog Denton pushed through the crowd and said quietly, "That'll be enough of that, McSween."

When Mulvane turned to look, he noticed that the Sheriff of Boulder City had his gun drawn and the muzzle lined on big Jehu McSween.

McSween turned to look at him, and then he said, "You're a damned fool, Denton, and always was. You know I've got more than a dozen gunhands in this town — and there's only one of you."

Mulvane had been standing about ten feet away from Denton, but he edged over in Denton's direction and said casually, "Two, Mr. McSween."

Jehu McSween's eyes narrowed as he looked at Mulvane. "You're another damned fool," he said.

Mulvane just shrugged and smiled.

Rog Denton was saying, "I'll take those two men, McSween. Have them cut loose. If you want to bring formal charges against them, you'll know where to find me."

McSween stood in the road, the bull-whip still in his hands. He looked at Denton and then at the two Harmon riders. Then he snapped, "Hell with you and your formal charges. Cut 'em loose, boys." As he passed by Denton, pushing through the crowd, he said, "Some day we'll run across these two up in the hills, Denton, and then we'll use more than a whip."

Rog Denton didn't answer him. They watched McSween and his riders move out of town, and Denton said to Mulvane, lounging out in front of the Cattleman's Bar, "I'm obliged, Mulvane."

Mulvane shrugged. "I don't like twelve to one," he said. "Didn't figure McSween would go as far as shooting down the law of Boulder City." He paused and then added thoughtfully, "One thing I can't figure out tonight, Sheriff."

"What's that?" Denton asked.

"Where in hell was Harmon?"

Denton shook his head. "Reckon Bannerman lost his guts, too, when he saw McSween come in here with a dozen men. He skipped out."

Mulvane wondered about Bannerman, too. Why had Bannerman gone into the alley? Why had he wanted to knock down one of McSween's men, and why hadn't he rounded up the Circle H riders when he suspected that McSween would be heading in to Boulder City? There were a great many why's about Griff Bannerman, and Mulvane didn't like any of them.

Rog Denton was saying sourly, "Whole damned business is heading for a blow-up."

"Step aside," Mulvane advised, "and let it blow, Sheriff."

"You don't wear the star around here," Denton growled.

That night Mulvane rode back to Slash E with Stub McCabe and Dave Shaw, and it was well past midnight when they turned in to the bunkhouse. McCabe had absorbed quite a bit of liquor, and he was in a happy mood. He started to sing as he kicked off his boots, and Mulvane tried to shut him up, thinking of Rosslyn Elder asleep back in the darkened ranch house.

Since McCabe had made a lot of noise unsaddling his horse, Mulvane was not too surprised when he heard Rosslyn's voice outside the door.

"Mulvane," she was saying.

Dave Shaw looked at Mulvane and then up at the ceiling, and he grinned.

Mulvane stepped to the door, opened it and went out. He found the girl standing a few yards from the door, her back half turned toward him. The night was cool, and a full moon sailed up in the sky. She was clearly illuminated in the bright light, her figure tall, slim and erect, her shoulders stiff. She said caustically, "I'm paying you a very good salary, Mulvane. Is that not right?"

Mulvane smiled. "Guess that's right."

"When I pay you a big salary," the girl went on grimly, "I expect you to be on the premises occasionally."

"Reckon I was on the premises, yesterday," Mulvane reminded her, "when I pushed that flock of sheep to hell out of your valley. You want any more than that?"

Rosslyn Elder was silent a moment. "You've been gone since morning," she said sulkily.

Mulvane said, "You're not paying me to sit out in front of this bunkhouse and watch your stock."

"What did you do today for your money?" Rosslyn asked him tersely.

Mulvane leaned back against the wall of the bunkhouse, took out his packet of tobacco and rolled a cigarette. Then he said easily, "Saw Jehu McSween, shot and killed two of McSween's riders. Saw John Ames in Boulder City and warned him to keep the hell out of Pleasant Valley. That enough for you for one day?"

Rosslyn turned to look at him again. She said, "Why did you want to see McSween?"

"Figured I'd like to know where he stood as far as Pleasant Valley was concerned," Mulvane told her. "He's out of it. If Ames tries to run his woolies into the valley, he does it on his own."

"What about the McSween riders?" the girl asked him.

Mulvane shrugged. "Those two dogs jumped me my first day over the pass," he explained. "I owed them something, and they figured they owed me something back. They tried to pay off today, and they lost."

Rosslyn said, "It would appear that I've hired the right man."

Mulvane nodded. He puffed on the cigarette, then said, "Ames had a message for you, too. He said that if he's being warned to keep his sheep out of Pleasant Valley, you'd better see to it that your beef doesn't move out of it. He sounds like a man who means what he says."

Rosslyn said petulantly, "There's no one in those hills telling me where I can graze my stock."

She turned and walked back toward the house, and Mulvane crushed out his cigarette, tossed it away and turned in for the night.

In the morning he was currying the claybank when Boyd Harmon and four of his riders came in to Pleasant Valley driving three hundred head of Circle H beef ahead of them.

Harmon came on to the house as the Circle H men, aided now by the three Slash E riders, pushed the stock deeper into the valley. The Circle H rancher passed near the stable where Mulvane was working. Harmon just looked at him and kept going.

Watching from the stable as he worked, Mulvane saw Rosslyn Elder come out and speak with Harmon, and then both of them went into the house.

The Circle H men came back to the bunkhouse and sat around smoking and passing the time of day with Shaw, McCabe and Bannion. Mulvane finally finished with the claybank and passed two of them squatting on their heels near the bunkhouse door.

He said to them as he paused, "Didn't see you two boys in Boulder last night for the party."

The Circle H riders looked at him and then looked away.

"Didn't know a damned thing about it," one of them said sourly.

"Griff Bannerman knew," Mulvane told him, "and then he skipped out when McSween came in."

Behind him, Mulvane heard the ranch door open, and then Boyd Harmon and Rosslyn Elder came out. Mulvane leaned back against the wall of the bunkhouse, watching Harmon come up. He didn't doubt that Rosslyn had informed Harmon of Mulvane's actions the past day or two, and, watching the big Circle H rancher come toward them now, Mulvane wondered idly what kind of relationship existed between these two.

Harmon pulled up in front of Mulvane and said flatly, "Like a word with you, Mulvane."

Mulvane shrugged. "Talk is cheap," he said. "Go ahead."

"Over here," Harmon growled, and he turned and walked toward the corral.

Mulvane took his time following. He flipped away the cigarette he'd been smoking, and then he strolled leisurely past the watching riders, winking broadly at Dave Shaw as he went by.

Harmon turned to face Mulvane, and Mulvane could see the anger in his green eyes. Harmon had a tough, uncompromising chin, and he thrust it out as he started to talk.

"I understand Ames told you to keep Slash E beef in the valley," he said. "That right?"

Mulvane nodded. "You heard right."

"And," Harmon went on, "Miss Elder informs me you won't be backing her if she tries to graze beef out beyond the valley on range that rightfully belongs to her."

Mulvane smiled. "What belongs to her and what belongs to the sheepmen are two different things. I didn't come to this part of the country to decide."

"You signed on with Slash E," Harmon snapped at him. "That means you back up every move Slash E might make."

Mulvane shook his head. "Not me," he said. "My job is in Pleasant Valley. Miss Elder knows that."

"McSween scare you off?" Harmon sneered.

Mulvane looked at him. "Kind of scared you off last night, Harmon," he said. "Where in hell were you when McSween came in to Boulder looking for your riders?"

Harmon glared at him. "I didn't know a damned thing about it until this morning," he said.

Mulvane was positive the man was speaking the truth. "Bannerman knew about it," he said. "You didn't. You run Circle H or does Bannerman?"

Harmon scowled. "Bannerman figured he could handle it alone, until he saw how many men McSween had with him."

"I still figure you weren't too anxious to ride in," Mulvane said easily.

Harmon said softly, "You're pretty rough with your tongue, mister."

Mulvane said, "You weren't too tough last night, Harmon, any way you look at it."

"Take off that gunbelt," Harmon said sharply.

Mulvane smiled. "My pleasure." He unbuckled the belt and draped it over a rail of the corral.

Harmon took off his gunbelt, too, placing it on the ground nearby. He tossed his hat on top of the belt and said, "Come and get it, mister."

As Mulvane took off his hat and the leather jacket he'd been wearing that morning, he saw Rosslyn Elder standing on the porch watching them, and he wondered whether she'd goaded Boyd Harmon into this.

The Slash E and Circle H riders were watching from the bunkhouse, and as Mulvane put his hat and jacket on the ground he saw Dave Shaw toss a coin into the air, and he knew that Shaw was trying to get a wager on the outcome.

"Ready?" Harmon asked.

"Don't be so damned polite." Mulvane grinned. "This is not going to be a polite fight."

Harmon came at him, then, slightly taller and considerably heavier than Mulvane, with solid shoulders and a thick neck. A man built like this would take an awful lot of whipping before he gave in.

The Circle H rancher tried to rush Mulvane against the wall of the corral, but Mulvane moved away from him and then stepped in fast, swinging hard with both fists, some of his blows landing on Harmon's arms and others getting through to his face.

Mulvane punched savagely for several moments, drawing first blood from Harmon's mouth. Then, as the bigger man righted himself and charged in like a wild man, Mulvane gave ground. This was the way he intended to fight — to drive in and slash like a wolf, and then give way, only to move in again when Harmon slowed down.

But Boyd Harmon was much faster on his feet than Mulvane had anticipated. He maneuvered Mulvane against the corral fence, pushing him hard and then smashing several heavy blows to the face.

Mulvane felt his knees buckle, and he grasped Harmon around the waist to prevent himself from falling to the ground. Harmon slashed at him savagely, trying to throw him off and get at him again, but Mulvane clung to him until his head was clearer, and then, instead of backing away, he slammed his right fist hard into Harmon's stomach.

Harmon stepped back, gasping for air, and then Mulvane rushed in at him, swinging hard for his face again, knocking him backward. Harmon's legs became entangled, and he went down. He got up immediately, cursing, and tore back in at Mulvane.

This time Mulvane was waiting for him, and the two men stood toe to toe, swinging at each other, before a hard blow to Mulvane's temple knocked him backward to a sitting position on the ground.

Grinning, he got to his feet, and then Harmon rushed him, pinning him back against the corral rails. As the rancher tried to smash with his fists, Mulvane lurched away from the fence, retreating as Harmon followed him.

Harmon was too anxious now, and he came in wide open. As he did so, Mulvane pulled up, dug his heels into the dirt, bent low and came up swinging a hard, full blow at Harmon's stomach.

This time the Circle H owner dropped to his knees, his mouth wide open, gagging for air. Blood dripped from his chin and mouth.

Mulvane's face had been cut in several places, too, and he could feel blood trickling down from his right cheekbone. He moved over to the corral and leaned against one of the posts, breathing heavily, waiting for Harmon to get up. He knew very definitely that the fight had only begun.

As he stood there for a moment, he glanced over at Rosslyn Elder on the porch and saw the animosity in her eyes.

Harmon got up, taking his time about it, and Mulvane said amiably, "You're a damned hard man to convince, Harmon."

Harmon said nothing. He came in again now, a little more cautiously, but he came in, his big fists clenched. The first time he hit Mulvane he knocked him sprawling, ten feet away.

Groggily, Mulvane got to his feet, amazed at the strength of the big rancher. He'd thought he'd had Harmon on the way, but now the rancher seemed to be stronger than ever.

Mulvane managed to evade Harmon's next rush, but a short while later a flurry of punches to the head and face knocked him to his knees again. He got up this time, with blood trickling from his battered mouth, and realized that it could be a very long fight.

"Give it up —" Harmon was breathing heavily — "or I might kill you, mister."

"I'll take a hell of a lot of killing," Mulvane mumbled, and he rushed in, driving Harmon before him, knocking him back into a horse trough, and then stumbling over the trough himself. Both men rolled on the ground.

Harmon lunged in again at Mulvane, trying to corner him against the corral, but Mulvane managed to keep away from him. He circled warily and then leaped in again, fists slashing at Harmon's face. He tore open the corner of Harmon's right eye, but Harmon did not even seem to notice it.

With blood cascading down the side of his face, Harmon tore in at Mulvane with hard, heavy blows. One of them got through Mulvane's guard, caught him in the ribs and tumbled him into the dust again.

Climbing to his feet, Mulvane wondered if he'd had any ribs cracked from that heavy blow to the side. As Harmon came in, Mulvane crouched and brought his fist up hard to Harmon's stomach. It was another full, swinging blow, even harder than the first one he'd slammed into Harmon's mid-section.

The rancher sagged, his hands dropping to his sides and his mouth wide open, and then Mulvane went at him savagely. He struck at least a dozen blows to Harmon's face and head, knocking him against the corral wall, but Harmon would not go down. He stood there, gagging, still unable to raise his hands as Mulvane continued to slam home the blows.

Harmon lay back against the corral logs, his arms spread out to support himself, and Mulvane knew that he would not go down even though he was battered into a state of unconsciousness. A man like this would stay on his feet until he was dead. When Mulvane realized this, he turned away, leaving Harmon still sagging against the corral.

Walking back to the bunkhouse, he said to one of Harmon's riders, "Better get him into the house and wash him up."

As the Harmon man walked to the corral, Mulvane looked at Rosslyn Elder on the porch. She was still in the same place, looking down at him, her face expressionless.

Little Dave Shaw went for a pail of water for Mulvane as he moved over to the porch. He stood there, breathing hard, feeling the pain now in his face and body. He said to the girl, "Like it?"

Rosslyn Elder just glared at him.

Shaw was waiting with the bucket of water. Rosslyn Elder called to the little rider, and Shaw put down the water and came toward the porch.

When he came up, Rosslyn said to him evenly, "We're moving that new bunch of beeves up into the hills this afternoon, Dave."

Shaw blinked, and Mulvane smiled despite the pain it gave him.

"What hills?" Shaw asked foolishly.

"You know damn well what hills," Rosslyn snapped. "West of Pleasant Valley."

Dave Shaw looked at Mulvane.

"I'm out of it," Mulvane said.

Shaw scowled, and the girl said to him, "You going to obey orders, Dave, or do you want your pay now?"

Shaw grinned. "Hell, Slash E is my brand, Miss Elder. You want them beeves up in the hills, they'll go in the hills. What the hell happens to 'em is not my fault."

Mulvane dabbed at his cut lips with a handkerchief. He said to Rosslyn, "Reckon you can send me a draft for whatever you think you owe me to the Boulder City Hotel."

"How much?" Rosslyn snapped.

Mulvane shrugged. "Whatever you think it's worth," he said. Then he turned and walked away.

The Circle H rider was leading the still dazed and battered Boyd Harmon up to the house when Mulvane walked back to the bunkhouse. Inside, Dave Shaw got a towel and helped him wash the blood from his face.

"You gave him a hell of a beating," Shaw said, "an' now I reckon you're through at Slash E."

Mulvane nodded. "If you three boys are smart, you'll run her stock into the hills and then duck."

Shaw grinned. "Aim to. I ain't takin' no lead from McSween's toughs just so's Rosslyn Elder kin raise beef on land she's never used."

Mulvane had his dinner in the bunkhouse, and when he came out to saddle up the claybank he noticed that Harmon and the Circle H riders were gone.

Bannion grinned coldly. "He didn't look too good. You worked over him, Mulvane."

Mulvane didn't see Rosslyn Elder about as he stepped into the saddle and headed back toward Boulder City, but he supposed it was just as well. He had thought she was going to prove quite interesting, and she'd turned out to be only mercenary. In a man he might overlook such a fault; in a woman it was unpardonable.

CHAPTER
TEN

It was mid-afternoon when he reached Boulder City and registered again at the hotel, leaving the claybank at the stables in back.

He went up to his room after registering, and as he changed his shirt, he wondered whether he should see a doctor about his ribs, which were blue and bruised from Harmon's hard fists.

When he came downstairs at suppertime, the clerk said to him, "Letter for you, Mr. Mulvane. A Slash E rider brought it in."

Mulvane picked up the letter, and when he opened it he found a draft in it for one hundred dollars, signed by Rosslyn Elder. He had no objections to the fee.

Slipping the draft into his shirt pocket, he headed down toward the restaurant for his supper. As he passed the sheriff's office, Denton came out, hooked a finger at him, and said, "Hear you walked out on Slash E."

Mulvane smiled. "You hear things pretty quick in this town."

"Couldn't get along with Miss Elder?" Denton asked him.

"Not when she figures on moving cattle up into McSween's hills," Mulvane said, "and expects me to back her bluff with a gun."

Rog Denton frowned. "That what she's up to?" he asked slowly.

"Three hundred head of Circle H stock were moved into Pleasant Valley this morning," Mulvane told him. "Miss Elder gave her riders orders to move the fresh stock west, up into the hills."

"That should bring it to a head," Denton growled, "if that's what they've been after all this time. McSween will back Ames, and Harmon will back Rosslyn, along with the other ranchers. The war is on."

Mulvane grinned. "What the hell you been having all this time before? Both the cattlemen and the sheep raisers in this part of the country must be laying out half their profits to pay for their hired guns."

"Who are you latched on to now?" Denton asked.

"Nobody." Mulvane smiled. "You still paying railroad wages for that deputy job, Sheriff?"

"You know what the pay is," Denton said, "and there's damn little chance that it will go up." He paused and then he said, "You riding on now that you're out of this?"

Mulvane shrugged. "No hurry," he said. He intended to stay, at least for a while, because there was still a possibility that U. P. Mulvane would show up in Boulder, and Mulvane was more than a little curious to meet his older brother.

"I told you before," Denton warned him. "The man who sits up on the fence in this town is between two fighting dogs."

102

"Been around fighting dogs before." Mulvane laughed and walked on to the restaurant.

An hour later, as he came out and was standing on the walk, he saw Griff Bannerman coming into town riding a chestnut horse. Bannerman turned the horse in his direction and pulled up in front of Mulvane.

The Circle H ramrod was smiling affably as usual, and he said, "Hear you had a little excitement in town last night after I left."

"You left in a hell of a hurry," Mulvane told him coldly.

Bannerman shrugged. "Saw how many riders McSween had," he said, "and I thought I'd get to hell out to Circle H and see if I could round up some of our boys."

Mulvane nodded without saying anything.

"Kind of run over my boss this morning, too, didn't you?" Bannerman said, grinning.

Mulvane said, "What is it you want to know, Bannerman?"

The Circle H foreman shrugged. "Passin' the time of day," he said.

"Pass it with someone else," Mulvane told him, and he moved on down the street toward the Cattleman's Bar.

"Figured there was something else you'd like to know," Bannerman called after him, and Mulvane pulled up, waiting.

Bannerman came down in his direction, pulled up again and said, "You heard Miss Elder was going to put some beef up into the hills west of Pleasant Valley?"

Mulvane nodded.

"She tried it this afternoon," Bannerman told him, "an' she run into a hornet's nest. Bunch of riders waiting for her drove her stock from here to hell an' back. Chased her riders clean back to the Slash E bunkhouse."

Mulvane considered this information for the moment. He'd driven Ames' riders out of the country, which meant that this time McSween's riders had been doing the driving. Ames had apparently tipped off McSween that there was to be an invasion by the cattlemen. How had Ames known that Rosslyn Elder intended to run her stock out of the Valley that afternoon?

"Anybody shot up?" Mulvane asked.

Bannerman shook his head. "A dozen McSween boys just turned the stock back, scattering them all over the countryside. Take Miss Elder a week to pick up those three hundred head she just bought from Harmon."

"She had it coming," Mulvane said, and he turned and walked away.

He sat in at a card game the early part of the evening, but there was restlessness running through him again tonight, and the cards bored him. After a while he pulled out of the game, bought a cigar at the bar and went out on the porch of the Cattleman's Bar to smoke it.

John Fogarty came out and said, "The luck running against you, Mulvane?"

Mulvane shrugged as he sat down in a wicker chair on the porch and put his boots up on the rail.

"When a man's luck runs out," Fogarty went on sagely, "and he don't care for the cards, it's time he moved on."

Mulvane had been thinking that, too. There was a good possibility that his brother would never turn up in the town and that he would waste a month of his life sitting on this porch waiting for him. Logically, it was time to move on. But there was a thread of curiosity running through him, too. He was now out of the sheepman-cattleman war, but he knew all of the contesting parties, and he was curious to see who would come out on top. McSween had just chased Rosslyn Elder's stock out of the mountains; the next move was up to Harmon and the cattlemen.

Sitting on the porch, he saw Griff Bannerman go by, and minutes later Sheriff Denton, walking with that stoop-shouldered walk, angled across the street, looked in at the Oriental Bar and then moved on up the street, making his rounds.

The night was hot and still, and, as occasional riders went by, the dust particles kicked up by their horses' hoofs hung in the air, glittering like diamonds in the light from the saloons.

Idly, Mulvane wondered whether Harmon was now organizing a war party to go into the hills after McSween, and, if he was, what in hell Bannerman was doing in town.

It was about midnight when Mulvane got up from his chair, tossed away the stub of cigar and headed up the street toward the hotel. He was going up the stairs to his room when he heard the single shot at the east end of town.

Pausing on the stairs, he waited, listening but hearing no further shots. He was about to shrug it off, thinking that perhaps some drunken cowpoke had fired at the moon, when he heard a man running by outside, yelling at the top of his voice.

"They got Rog Denton!"

His jaw tight, Mulvane swung around and headed downstairs again. When he reached the street, people were already running past the hotel front heading toward the east end of town. As Mulvane moved with them he saw a group of men approaching, carrying a body.

"Denton ain't dead," a man was saying. "Got a bullet in the back. They're takin' him to Doc Partridge's."

Mulvane hooked a finger in the coat lapel of a man moving by, turned him around and asked, "They see who did it?"

"Bushwhacked," the townsman growled. "Rog was saddlin' his horse in the Emerald Livery when he got it in the back. Reckon somebody fired at him from the door."

Mulvane thought about this. It was a strange hour for Rog Denton to be riding out of town, and the fact that he'd been shot as he was saddling up would seem to indicate that he'd been shot to prevent him from leaving town.

After they'd gone by with Rog Denton's body, Mulvane walked idly down to the Emerald Livery

Stable. The hostler had taken the saddle from Denton's big bay horse, and he was leading the animal back into a stall when Mulvane came in.

The hostler, a little man with a lame leg, limped back from the stall, shaking his head as he saw Mulvane in the doorway. Expecting questions, he said, "I was sleepin' up in the loft when I heard the shot. Rog was layin' on the floor, an' there wasn't nobody around."

Mulvane heard a step behind him, and when he turned around he saw Griff Bannerman moving into the lamplight.

Bannerman shook his head and said, "Who in hell would want to shoot Denton?"

Mulvane said casually, "Maybe the same man tried to do in Jehu McSween."

Bannerman was standing less than two feet away, and Mulvane reached out with his hand. Before the surprised Bannerman could object or pull back, Mulvane had slipped Bannerman's gun from the holster, broken it and examined the charges. There were five slugs in the cylinder of the Colt .44, the hammer resting on the empty chamber.

"Not me," Bannerman said, grinning. "Always liked Denton."

Mulvane smiled. "Would that stop you from shooting him?"

Bannerman shrugged. "No damned reason to shoot Rog," he said, and he held out his hand for the gun.

Mulvane gave it back to him.

"Bad business," Bannerman observed, "takin' a gun from a man."

"You didn't do anything about it," Mulvane said, and he turned and left the stable.

He was up in his room ten minutes later when a knock sounded on the door. When he opened it, a short, heavy-set man named Anderson, with whom he'd played cards that evening, was waiting outside. Anderson was the owner of the local feed store.

"You're not sleepin' yet," Anderson observed. "Rog Denton wants to see you, Mulvane."

"How is he?" Mulvane asked.

Anderson shrugged. "Doc got the bullet out. Missed his spine, but he'll be laid up for a month or two. You want to step over?"

Mulvane buckled on his gunbelt and reached for his hat. "Know what he wants?" he asked.

"Have an idea," Anderson said succinctly. "Let him tell you, Mulvane."

They crossed the street to the physician's office, which was on the second floor above Anderson's store. Rog Denton lay in a back room, his face grayer than ever and the pain still in his eyes.

"Sit down," he said when Mulvane came in.

"Know who did it?" Mulvane asked him.

Denton shook his head. "Shot in the dark," he said. "Reckon a man should never have his back to a door when he's wearing the star."

Mulvane sat twirling his hat idly in his hands. "Must have had a good reason to shoot you."

"They did," Denton told him flatly. "I was headed out to the McSween place to warn him that more than fifty riders were going up into the hills tomorrow to smash him. I got that from a Harmon rider who just quit his job."

Mulvane thought about that. "McSween can handle them," he said.

Denton scowled. "Not that many. This is a full scale war now. I wanted to warn McSween, and then I figured on stopping Harmon before the lead started to fly."

"And you walked into lead yourself," Mulvane said. "You're a damned fool, Denton."

"I'm a lawman," Denton told him thinly. "You wear the star, you take on certain responsibilities."

Mulvane didn't say anything, still wondering why Denton had wanted to see him at this hour of the night.

"Reckon I'll be laid up for a good many weeks," Denton was saying quietly. "Town's going to need a lawman. I'm asking you, Mulvane."

Mulvane looked at him. "Turned you down before," he said.

"Different now," Rog Denton stated. "Nobody else in this town has the nerve to wear this star, the way things are shaping up. Figured I'd ask you. You can ride to hell out of here now, Mulvane, but when you ride keep remembering that there's going to be a lot of innocent people shot up unless someone stops it."

"Way you put it," Mulvane said, "a man would think I'd started this thing."

"Nobody really starts a war," Denton said quietly, "and I'm convinced that nobody wants this one, but it's here. If Harmon's riders go busting out to the

McSween place tomorrow, there'll be hell to pay. There are women and children out there, too, you know."

Mulvane remembered then that Charity McSween was out at the McSween place. She had saved his life. A man could not be a man and forget that.

"Pin that star on," Sheriff Denton told him, "and then ride out to McSween's and warn him. Then see if you can talk some sense into Harmon."

"Hell of a big order." Mulvane grinned, but he picked up the star from the dresser where it lay and tossed it up into the air. When it landed in the palm of his hand, face up, he said casually, "Swear me in, Denton."

He'd done foolish things in the past, and he probably would do more foolish things in the future before that final bullet caught up with him, but at the moment he could not remember anything that had made less sense than this. He tried to console himself with the thought that he was doing it for Charity McSween.

CHAPTER
ELEVEN

Riding the claybank gelding out through the back alleys of Boulder City fifteen minutes later, Mulvane wondered how long he could stay alive caught between two opposing factions, neither one of which had any use for him. He'd saddled the claybank surreptitiously, after having gone down the back stairway from the hotel after leaving Rog Denton. He hoped that the ones who'd shot down Denton would not know that a new man wore the star until he was well up into the hills.

He was less than half a mile from town when he knew that he hadn't fooled anyone. Very distinctly, he heard riders coming up behind him, fanning out as they approached to cut him off if he attempted to swerve to either side.

Leaning forward in the saddle, Mulvane touched his spurs to the claybank, and the big horse shot ahead. He was confident that, barring any unforeseen happenings, the big gelding could outrace any horse in this part of the country.

They were moving up the trace that led into the foothills and the mountains beyond, and as Mulvane rode on at top speed he could hear his pursuers falling behind. Once in the foothills he was positive he could lose the men behind him, but out here in open country it was impossible.

He wasn't going to make the foothills, though. Up ahead of him he caught the glint of moonlight on a rifle barrel, and he knew, then, that he was riding straight into an ambush. He first thought of cutting away to either side, swinging away from the men in front of him and his pursuers, but already the riders coming on behind had swung out wide.

There was another choice, and he accepted it unhesitatingly, while fully recognizing its dangers. Pulling up the claybank suddenly, he jerked the animal around and headed straight back toward his pursuers. He rode at top speed now, hanging over the side of the saddle and holding his gun in his hand.

The riders behind him had been about a hundred yards to the rear, and they were still moving at top speed when Mulvane swung around and drove back at them. In the dim light he could see two of them still in the road, with the other two thirty or forty yards out on either side. As he drove the big claybank back toward Boulder City, the two men in the road pulled up their horses in confusion. He was on top of them in a moment, the big gelding roaring past.

A gun roared as he hung even farther down on the side of the saddle away from the two riders. Half under the gelding's neck, he threw one quick shot, not expecting to hit anyone from this position but knowing that the shot would momentarily divert them.

He raced on, hearing more shots coming after him as he headed back toward the distant lights of Boulder

City. Had he so desired, he could have reached the town in safety without any difficulty, but tonight he had set out for the McSween place, and he intended to reach it.

Halfway back to Boulder he swung off the road again, and, turning into a clump of cottonwoods, he dismounted and waited, listening for sounds of pursuit. But the men who had tried to bushwhack him had not followed him when he changed directions.

He remained in the cottonwood grove for about thirty minutes, smoking a cigarette, keeping the glowing tip concealed as he squatted on his heels at the edge of the grove. There was no movement on the road leading from Boulder City up into the hills.

In the darkness he'd had no opportunity to see who had tried to set him up here tonight, but he had little doubt that the same man or men who had shot down Rog Denton had been laying for him, too. They'd watched him go up to Denton's room, and they'd seen him ride out of Boulder, even though he'd gone out through back alleys. Whoever had tried to bushwhack him tonight was still out in the hills, waiting to make sure that he did not get through to McSween.

After a while, tossing the cigarette butt away, he stepped into the saddle again. This time he turned the claybank due north and rode parallel with the mountains. It was impossible to reach McSween by taking the trace out to his place, but there were other ways of getting into these mountains.

He pushed on for about three miles toward the north, and then he turned in among the foothills and climbed gradually until he reached the timber-line. He had gone about two thousand feet up into the mountains when he ran across his first sheep herd, a mass of dull white spread out across a wood-enclosed meadow.

At the far end of the meadow he saw the herder's round-topped wagon, and the dog, catching his scent and hearing the horse approach, began to bark. Mulvane skirted the sheep flock and approached the wagon carefully.

A bearded man in his undershirt, with a rifle in his hands, appeared in the rear opening of the wagon, and called gruffly, "Who in hell is this?"

"Hold it up," Mulvane said, and then he grinned and added, "this is the sheriff."

"You ain't Rog Denton," the sheepherder said suspiciously as Mulvane came up to the wagon astride the claybank.

"Denton's been shot back in Boulder City," Mulvane explained. "Reckon I'm wearing the star now, mister. I'm looking for McSween's place."

"You could be one o' them damned ranchers tryin' to find your way through past our guards," the herder told him grimly, "an' how in hell would I know?"

Mulvane struck a match and held it on the star pinned to his vest. "Reckon you'd better show me the quickest way up to McSween's place," he said quietly, "or McSween will skin your hide in the morning. There are fifty gunthrowers heading this way tomorrow, and McSween has to know."

114

The herder paused, scratched his head and then said, "Looks like you're alone, mister. Reckon you can't do too much harm even if that star is faked."

He came out of the wagon then and kicked up his fire, pushing the coffeepot on the coals. In a short while he poured Mulvane a steaming hot cup while Mulvane told him about the shooting of Rog Denton back in Boulder City, and of the attempt to bushwhack him as he rode up the trace.

Finishing his coffee, Mulvane stepped into the saddle, and the herder saddled a mule he kept tied to the wagon. They rode due west, pushing up into the hills, finding trails where Mulvane would never have expected them to exist.

They moved up higher and higher into the mountains, and Mulvane figured that they had been riding for about an hour when he spotted the light from the house up ahead.

"There she is," the herder told him, "an' old Jehu's liable to blow your head off for bustin' in on him at this hour of the night."

"Take my chances." Mulvane grinned and rode on alone.

He figured the time to be about three o'clock in the morning when he came up on the porch of the McSween house and banged on the door with his gun butt.

A Chinese cook opened the door after a matter of minutes and stared at Mulvane stupidly. Then Jehu McSween boomed from behind him, "Who in hell is that at this hour of the night."

"Mulvane. Strike a light."

The lamp inside was turned up, and Mulvane stepped into the house. McSween had pulled on his pants and boots, but the sleep was still in his eyes as he stared at Mulvane.

"Reckon you didn't come here for a social visit," the big sheepherder said grimly, his pale blue eyes shifting to the star on Mulvane's vest. "And it looks to me like you've been changing jobs since I last saw you."

Briefly, Mulvane told him about the shooting of Denton, and of Denton's request that he wear the star and ride up here to warn the sheepmen.

"About fifty gunthrowers coming into these hills in the morning," Mulvane told him. "Denton figured you ought to know before they bust you up."

McSween thought about that for a moment. Then he said quietly, "They'll outnumber us, but we'll know how to handle them up here in the hills. Reckon I'm obliged to you, Mulvane."

Mulvane grinned coldly. "My job is to prevent killings."

"Which means that you've changed a hell of a lot in a short time," Jehu McSween observed. "Where do you fit in when Harmon's bunch comes up this way?"

Mulvane shrugged. "I might try talking to Harmon," he said.

"Reckon you didn't get much chance to talk tonight," McSween told him grimly. "If this bunch is coming up here for blood, they're not stopping because of you."

116

Mulvane knew that, too, but he'd promised Rog Denton to make an attempt to stop the fight.

"You can bed down here," McSween was saying, "or out at the bunkhouse."

Mulvane chose the bunkhouse, taking one of the bunks near the door after he'd stabled the claybank. He slept three hours, and when he awoke he discovered that McSween was already busy setting fortifications around the ranch house. They'd overturned a few wagons, and were now piling sand bags and bales of hay against them. Heavy, loop-holed wooden shutters were being closed over all the windows.

There were about a dozen men around the premises, and McSween assured him that others were riding in to assist if Harmon attacked here.

In the kitchen of the ranch house Charity served him coffee, bacon and biscuits, and she said quietly as she poured the coffee, "We're obliged to you for coming here, Mr. Mulvane."

"My pleasure," Mulvane assured her.

"You seem to be changing jobs quite swiftly in this country," Charity observed, coolness in her voice, and Mulvane grinned up at her as she moved by him toward the stove. "Didn't you like working for Miss Elder?" Charity asked.

"Didn't like the way she treated the help." Mulvane smiled, and Charity turned to look at him curiously. Mulvane went on. "She was willing to see her men shot down so that she could have her way."

Charity didn't say anything, and when Mulvane finished he stepped outside and located her father. Jehu came bustling up, a rifle in his hand, and Mulvane said to him, "How many men do you have now?"

"Fifteen here," McSween told him. "Another dozen riding in."

"Not enough," Mulvane observed. "Those ranchers aren't coming up here with peashooters in their hands. They'll have two or three dozen gunfighters in their crew."

"We'll be ready for them," Jehu McSween said confidently.

Mulvane just shook his head. He saddled the claybank and rode down the mountain, wondering if Harmon and the other ranchers were now moving up into the hills.

The morning was half spent as he turned the claybank down the trace that led toward Boulder City. The morning was gray, with a mist still hanging in the valleys and the smell of rain in the air. When the mist became heavier, Mulvane unstrapped the oilskin from behind the saddle and put it on, pulling his hat brim low on his face.

He had gone less than a mile or so down the trace when he saw the column of smoke rising from a point off to his left. The smoke was too heavy for a campfire. It looked more as if a log cabin or, as Mulvane guessed immediately, a sheepwagon was going up in flames.

Turning the claybank off the trace, he rode in the direction of the smoke and ten minutes later emerged into a grassy meadow, which he now recognized as the one into which he'd stumbled the previous night trying to find the McSween place.

The sheepwagon was a smoldering ruin at the far end of the meadow. There were no sheep in the valley, and no barking dog. Grim-faced, Mulvane rode the claybank along the edge of the meadow to the burning wagon.

He saw the dog first, sprawled on the ground, dead — and then he spotted the herder only a few yards away, lying on his face, still in his undershirt. A rifle lay a few feet from him, and Mulvane assumed that he'd attempted to put up some kind of fight and had been shot down.

Dismounting, Mulvane went over to the herder, rolled him over and saw the bullet hole through his forehead. He threw a blanket over the body and then stepped back into the saddle.

Picking up the trail of the men who'd shot down the sheepherder took only a matter of minutes. They had evidently rounded up the band of sheep in the meadow and driven them off toward the north. Three riders had come into the quiet meadow, killed the herder and moved off with the sheep.

Mulvane followed them, loosening the Winchester rifle in the saddle holster as he did so. The sheep had been driven through the woods and then out onto a high plateau a mile or so beyond.

There were still no sheep in sight, and Mulvane could not even hear them. He frowned as he rode on across the plateau. Riding north, he spotted the thin column of smoke rising into the air that meant a campfire among the fringe of trees on the edge of the plateau. The three riders who had shot down the sheepherder were having a late breakfast.

As he rode across the plateau he noticed that it ascended rather sharply, and up ahead of him it seemed to break off. Even before he reached the far end, he knew what he would find.

Dismounting near the edge of a cliff wall, he moved forward on foot to look down. There was a drop of well over two hundred feet, and he saw the broken mass of white bodies below. The sheep had been deliberately driven over the cliff wall.

Pulling back from the edge of the precipice, Mulvane stepped into the saddle again and rode in the direction of the campfire, which was still concealed from him by the trees.

The mist was beginning to lift now, and before he reached the woods he took off the oilskin and tied it behind the saddle again. The campfire was another hundred yards beyond, in a small clearing.

Riding the claybank over beds of soft pine needles, Mulvane came upon the killers very suddenly. He walked the claybank out into the open and sat astride the horse, looking across at the men near the fire.

He did not know any of them. One man was tall and bony, with a narrow, pointed chin and a tuft of beard. He'd been sitting with a plate of bacon across his knees, but, when Mulvane walked the claybank into the clearing, he put the plate aside and stood up. He was wearing a pearl-handled Smith & Wesson on his hip.

The other two men were shorter and unprepossessing. One of them was on the fat side, with reddish hair, a round head and a very stubby nose. The third man had a harelip and a three days' growth of fuzzy black hair on his face.

The men stared at Mulvane speechlessly. Then Mulvane said gently, "When you boys finish your breakfast we'll ride back to Boulder City."

The tall man with the beard, who seemed to be the most dangerous of the three, wiped his hands on his pants and said, "What in hell for?"

Mulvane lifted his fingers to the badge on his vest. "Dead man back in the meadow a mile or so from here, and a couple of hundred sheep run over the cliff wall up ahead. Reckon you boys would like to tell somebody about that."

The man with the harelip spoke. "You ain't the sheriff of Boulder, mister. Seen him in town once."

Mulvane smiled. "New sheriff. Drop your gun-belts, boys."

The man with the harelip looked at the taller man, and then he spat and said, "You found a dead man back in the meadow, mister. That ain't any of our business."

Mulvane said, "Do your talking back in Boulder."

He knew they weren't coming without a fight, but, remembering the dead sheepherder back in the meadow, Mulvane was not too displeased.

The tall man grinned. "Three of us here, only one o' you, mister."

Mulvane said nothing. He sat astride the claybank, smiling at the three men in front of him.

"You ain't takin' us in," the tall man said again.

Mulvane said quietly, "You boys have three seconds to drop those gunbelts."

The bony man with the beard did not wait for the three seconds. He moved fast for the Smith & Wesson on his right hip, and the muzzle was clearing the holster when Mulvane's bullet struck him in the chest, knocking him back among the bushes on the other side of the fire.

Swiveling the gun, Mulvane said, "Hold it where it is, boys."

The harelipped man had started to go for his gun, too, but now dropped his hand. Both men stared at the tall fellow lying still among the bushes, face toward the sky.

Dismounting, gun still in hand, Mulvane walked around the fire, came up behind the two men and lifted their guns from the holsters, tossing them into the bushes. He looked at the dead man on the ground, then came around to the front of the fire again and said casually, "Sit down." He poured himself a cup of the coffee the bearded man would never drink.

As he sipped it he said to the men, "Where's Harmon?"

The harelipped man said sourly, "Hell with you, mister."

Mulvane had half a cup of hot coffee left. Without a word he threw the contents into the harelipped man's face, and the man let out a yell of pain as he staggered back, clutching at his face with both hands. He was cursing as he sat down on the ground, pawing at his face.

122

With his gun in one hand and the coffeepot in the other, Mulvane smiled down at the chubby man sitting in front of him. He said gently, "You like the whole pot in your face, Jack? I'm asking again — where's Harmon?"

The chubby man looked at the dead man in the bushes, and then he spat into the fire and said, "Them damned ranchers are still back in Boulder, mister. Sent some of us up into these hills to hit at the sheep."

"They aim to come up later?" Mulvane asked him.

The chubby man scowled. "Reckon that was the idea. They were waitin' for more gunthrowers to come in."

Mulvane thought about this. It was going to be a shock to Boyd Harmon when the new sheriff rode back into Boulder escorting his two prisoners.

After a while he had the two prisoners tie the dead man across the saddle of his horse, and then they all rode down the mountain, Mulvane in the rear.

They picked up the trace leading into Boulder, and, as they passed the spot where Mulvane had been waylaid the previous night, he said to the harelipped man, "You boys try to gun down a rider coming through here last night?"

"Wasn't even near Boulder last night," the harelipped man said sourly. "The three of us were out at Circle H."

This convinced Mulvane that it had been Griff Bannerman and a crew of his men who had been waiting for him along the trace. He realized that he owed Bannerman something that would have to be paid off sooner or later.

It was high noon when they rode in to Boulder City. Mulvane left the body of the dead man at the coroner's and then pushed down to the jailhouse. A crowd of men gathered around the jail as he took his prisoners inside, locking them in the cells at the rear.

When he came out again he spotted Rosslyn Elder standing on the porch of the Boulder City Hotel, looking in his direction. Boyd Harmon and Bannerman were supposed to be in town, but Mulvane had not seen either of them when he rode in.

Walking up toward the Cattleman's Bar, he met John Fogarty, and he said, "Harmon in town, John?"

"Rode out an hour or so ago," the floorman told him. "Had a big crew with him."

Mulvane frowned. Since he had not run across Harmon on the trace, this meant that the ranchers had taken a different route up into the mountains to avoid the sentinels McSween had set out.

"How many of them, John?" Mulvane asked.

"Fifteen or twenty," Fogarty said. "They were loaded for bear, Mr. Mulvane. You run into a little trouble yourself, back in the hills?"

"Real trouble coming up," Mulvane said, scowling, and he crossed the road and went up to see Rog Denton.

The sheriff of Boulder was slightly feverish, but he was able to recognize Mulvane and speak to him coherently.

"Feel like hell," Denton growled, "but Doc Partridge says this is part of the healing process. They tell me you brought in some prisoners."

Mulvane told him about the killing up in the meadow, and of the two prisoners locked in the cell across the road.

"McSween is forting up, waiting for Harmon to come out to him," he said. "They tell me Harmon has already gone up into the hills. You figure I ought to ride after him now and tell both sides to drop their guns?"

Rog Denton stared up at the ceiling with bloodshot eyes. "Aside from Harmon," he said quietly, "I don't figure most of the ranchers are looking for too much trouble. Harmon's been pushing them from the start. If you got to him, you might stop the others, too."

"They tell me he had fifteen guns with him when he left town," Mulvane observed, "and another dozen or two up in the hills putting the fear into the sheepherders. One man can't ride against that, Denton."

Denton didn't say anything. He only shook his head in disgust.

"I'll ride back up this afternoon," Mulvane promised, "but I don't figure there's much I can do, Denton."

"I've sent a wire to the governor for help," Denton told him glumly, "but they couldn't get any troopers here before the end of the week, and by then it'll all be over, one way or the other."

Mulvane crossed back to the hotel for a change of clothes, and he frowned when he found Rosslyn Elder waiting for him outside his door. The girl said tersely, "They're going to cut you down if you go out into those hills, Mulvane."

Mulvane looked at her. "That bother you?" he asked.

"It's foolish of you to try to buck both Harmon and McSween," she told him.

Mulvane shrugged. "A lawman bucks whoever gets in his way," he said.

"You're not a lawman," Rosslyn said, "and we want you to keep out of this."

Mulvane chuckled. "Too late. I'm in it."

She bit her lips in anger. "The cattlemen of this county have posted a thousand dollars down at the bank," she said. "You're to pick it up on your way out of town."

Mulvane whistled softly. "They figure that's cheaper than killing me?" he asked.

"They can kill you, too," Rosslyn said grimly. "For your own sake, why don't you ride out of here now?"

"I made a man a promise," Mulvane told her. "Tell Harmon he can keep his money."

"You'll be dead before nightfall," Rosslyn snapped. "Why are you such a fool?"

"Born that way," Mulvane said, grinning, and he walked past her into his room. He closed the door behind him, but Rosslyn opened it and stepped into the room. She leaned her back against the door and watched him while he stripped off his shirt and put on a clean one.

"I've always liked you," she said, her voice soft.

"And you like Harmon, too," Mulvane told her. "You like anybody who can do you a favor. Off-hand I'd say you liked money better than either one of us."

"You're wrong there," Rosslyn told him.

Mulvane buckled on his gunbelt again. He said, "Right now you're in a bind. McSween has scattered your stock, and you know you can't move cattle even as far as the other end of your valley unless McSween is licked, and he'll take a hell of a lot of licking."

He turned to go, but Rosslyn stood there, barring his way. Then she put a hand out, touching his arm, and said softly, "I could use help again, Mulvane."

Mulvane smiled. "Not from me. Did Harmon pay you to say that, too?"

She lashed out at him with her hand, slapping him full across the face. He picked her up bodily and flung her to one side of the door. He said quietly, "End of the line for you, Miss Elder."

He felt no pity for her. She was a woman whose only interest in men lay in using them. It was power she wanted, and money, and she was beginning to realize now that she would never have even these.

CHAPTER
TWELVE

Down on the street Mulvane stepped into the restaurant for a late dinner, and as he ate he wondered whether the fireworks had started up in the hills as yet. And he asked himself what one man could do to prevent a range war such as this.

Finishing his meal, he stepped into the saddle and rode out of town again, not quite sure yet what his plans were. He knew only that he had to keep moving, hoping that there would be a possibility of contacting some of the ranchers who were not too bitter against McSween. The odd thought suddenly occurred to him that, if his brother U.P. were to appear on the scene, he would be signing up with the ranchers — and one of U.P.'s jobs might be to help hunt down the sheriff!

Leaving Boulder City this time, Mulvane avoided the trace altogether, taking the northerly route again and riding the low ridges so he could see in many directions at once.

Off to the west as he rode he could hear distant gunfire, and he knew that the battle had started. But he kept riding north, not wishing to run directly into Harmon's riders, who were now between McSween and himself.

He was positive that McSween could hold the ranchers off for a time, at least, so there was no particular rush for him to attempt to intervene. The crackling of guns continued for some time, spluttering and then dying out, and then starting up again.

He circled casually into the hills as the afternoon waned and the first faint stars came out. The moon was coming up when he hit upon the trace running north and south through the mountains. There were many such traces in these high hills, because the sheepmen kept moving their flocks from one valley to another. This trace probably led back south to the McSween place and north to another sheepman's quarters.

Mulvane remembered someone telling him that the Ames' place was some distance north of McSween's; it could very well be that the trace led out to John Ames' sheep ranch.

On an impulse Mulvane turned the claybank north. At the McSween place, now, both sides would be sitting on their arms, Harmon only hoping that McSween did not receive reinforcements.

Following the trace north was an easy matter, and for about thirty minutes Mulvane rode on easily as the moon lifted higher and higher into the sky. The night had turned cool again, and he was now wearing the windbreaker he'd wisely tied behind his saddle that afternoon.

The trace ended on the edge of a high mountain meadow, and part way down the west edge of the meadow he saw the lights of a house. As he dismounted he heard a horse whinny, and he pulled the claybank back in among the trees, holding the gelding's nose so that it could not call back.

The door of the house opened, and a man stood in the light for a moment, looking out and listening. After a while the door closed again. Mulvane moved the horse deeper into the woods, and tied the animal there. Then he moved forward on foot, keeping in among the trees on the edge of the meadow.

Beyond the house he saw sheep grazing, a dirty white clump of them bunched up for the night. Evidently, Harmon's raiders had not struck here.

Carefully, Mulvane moved closer to the house, coming up behind it. As he drew near he could see a horse shed, set back some distance from the house, with a few horses stamping restlessly inside.

Three horses were tied out in front of the house, and, as one of them moved into the light from the window, he saw the brand on the animal. It was a Circle H — Harmon's brand. Why would a Circle H rider be visiting here?

The house was a long, low, rambling affair similar to McSween's. There were several windows on either side, and Mulvane drew up close to one of them. He could hear voices inside, but it was impossible to ascertain what was being said. He thought, though, that he recognized Griff Bannerman's voice, and he was immediately on guard.

Very carefully, Mulvane raised himself so that he could look in through the window. There were four men in the room, and the man sitting at the table with his back toward the window was John Ames, the sheepman.

Griff Bannerman stood near the fireplace, striking a match to a cigar he'd just put in his mouth. The two men with him were Circle H riders whom Mulvane had seen in town. With the windows shut he could not hear what was being said, but the very fact that they were together, and on such amiable terms, could mean only one thing. Like Bannerman, John Ames had seemed to be constantly pushing things from the direction of the mountains. He'd run his sheep down into Pleasant Valley, deliberately causing trouble. Possibly, like Bannerman, he was trying to bring about a full-scale war here — a war that could ruin Jehu McSween and leave John Ames the kingpin up on the mountain.

Ames and Bannerman, working together, could keep things in a constant turmoil so there would never be any real peace between sheepman and rancher. Mulvane remembered now that it was Bannerman who had squatted in that alley opposite the Cattleman's Bar with his rifle lined on one of McSween's men. Bannerman had undoubtedly pushed the sheepherders around up in the hills and had run Circle H stock higher into the mountains than Harmon had even supposed. He'd done this deliberately in order to incite the wrath of Jehu McSween.

Griff Bannerman, then, was working a double cross on Harmon, hoping to wreck Circle H in this war so he would be the big winner. This was why Ames was not at the McSween place with the other sheepmen fighting off the ranchers and why his flocks were not being touched.

Mulvane crouched beside the wall of the building, knowing that he'd seen enough. If he could prove to Harmon now that there was a liaison between Bannerman and Ames, and that most of the trouble centered around them, there was a possibility that the big fight up in the hills could be stopped.

Very carefully now, Mulvane backed away from the building until he was back near the horse shed. The claybank lay concealed in the woods about two hundred yards farther down along the edge of the meadow. As Mulvane hurried down along the fringe of trees, one of the three horses out front whinnied again, and the door suddenly shot open, a sliver of yellow light stretching out toward the woods. The beam caught Mulvane fully for one brief moment.

The man in the doorway was Griff Bannerman, and Mulvane heard him yell suddenly. At the same moment Mulvane heard riders coming up the meadow from the direction of the claybank. He leaped back into the shadows quickly, and as he did so Bannerman's gun boomed, clipping leaves over Mulvane's head.

Running back past the horse sheds, Mulvane lunged in among the trees. Behind him he could hear Griff Bannerman sounding the alarm, calling loudly for the riders approaching to hurry it up.

On foot, and in these woods, Mulvane knew quite definitely that Bannerman would ferret him out shortly. There would be at least half a dozen horsemen riding through here, combing the area, and one of them would certainly stumble upon him.

Running at top speed, plunging through the woods, he cursed his luck.

He ran on hard, moving through the trees opposite the flock of sheep, which were bedded down for the night. Behind him he could hear riders coming on fast. In a matter of moments they would be upon him.

It was then that he thought about the sheep. The flock was a mass of dull white spread out across the north end of the meadow. Grinning at the thought, Mulvane suddenly stepped out from among the trees and walked without haste toward the nearest sheep. He walked in among the flock, careful not to frighten any of them. Then he sat down on the ground, stretched out and pulled his hat across his face. He was lying flat on his back when he heard the riders go by, not more than thirty feet away.

Bannerman was calling sharply, "Spread out — spread out. He couldn't have gone far."

The sheep around Mulvane moved restlessly as the riders swept by, but then they calmed down again. Mulvane lay there, completely relaxed, his hat pulled across his face and his gun in hand, ready for use if he needed it. He could hear the horsemen rocketing through the woods, and then, minutes later, they came back again.

Bannerman yelled, "Two of you boys ride across this meadow. He may have crossed over."

Mulvane heard the riders move past the outskirts of the flock as they crossed the meadow, and then there was silence again. Several times now riders crisscrossed the meadow, but none of them thought to move in among the flock of sheep.

He must have been among the sheep for nearly an hour when he heard the riders departing. Lying there completely relaxed, he'd nearly dozed off. After a while he sat up and looked back toward the ranch house, which was less than three hundred yards away. He noticed as he sat up that the light was still on in the house.

Sniffing the sheep with distaste, Mulvane moved back to the edge of the woods and waited there for several minutes, listening carefully. Then he started back toward the house. He was positive now that Bannerman and his riders had left, which meant that Ames would be alone. He decided to have a little talk with Ames.

Approaching the house, he noticed that the horses were indeed gone. When he looked in through the side window he saw Ames sitting on the edge of the bunk, taking off his boots.

Smiling, Mulvane moved around to the front door, lifting his gun from the holster. Then he kicked the door open and stepped inside. There was a rifle standing in a corner near the bunk. John Ames looked at it and then at the gun in Mulvane's hand. He smiled resignedly, making no move to go for the gun.

Mulvane moved into the room, closing the door with his boot, the gun still lined on Ames' chest. Ames was still smiling, revealing clean white teeth against the black mustache. There was a gleam in his black eyes.

He said casually, "I'm curious to know where you were hiding, Mulvane. They searched every foot of ground around here."

"They didn't look through your flock of sheep," Mulvane told him. He picked up the rifle near the bunk and tossed it into a corner.

"What is it you want?" Ames asked him.

"Like you to ride back with me to the McSween place," Mulvane said, "and tell Jehu what in hell you and Bannerman have been doing up in these hills all this time."

"What have I been doing?" Ames countered.

"You've been working with Bannerman to start a range war that would ruin both McSween and Harmon, while both of you sit out here waiting for them to knock each other over."

John Ames lifted his eyebrows slightly. He said softly, "You seem to have the whole deal figured out, Mulvane. Only one thing wrong."

"What's that?" Mulvane asked.

"Who in hell will believe you?"

"Bannerman was here with you tonight," Mulvane said.

"And who will believe that, either?"

Mulvane shrugged. "Reckon we can find out," he said. "Now pull on your boots."

Ames pulled on his boots, but he still sat where he was, on the edge of the bunk. Then he put a cigar in his mouth, lit it and said, "Supposing I refuse to go?"

Mulvane smiled. "I can put a bullet through your head."

"That wouldn't help you," Ames pointed out. "If I'm dead, you can never prove anything."

Mulvane shrugged. "Reckon you don't have to be dead for me to get you over to McSween's. I could crack this gun barrel across your skull, but then you'd have a lump on your head in the morning. Why not just come nice and easy? You'll feel better."

Ames shrugged and smiled. "You hold the good cards," he said. "What's the next move?"

"Step outside and saddle one of those horses in the shed."

The sheepman put on his fleece-lined jacket, picked up his hat and walked out the door. Mulvane took a lantern from a peg on the wall and handed it to him. They walked down toward the horse shed, and Mulvane stood in the doorway while Ames threw a saddle on a big chestnut mare.

Finding a piece of rope in the shed, Mulvane bound Ames' legs underneath the horse's belly.

Ames smiled. "I won't leave you."

"Reckon you won't," Mulvane told him. He led the horse out of the shed and walked the animal down to the spot where he'd concealed the claybank.

Stepping into the saddle, Mulvane motioned Ames on ahead of him, down the trace in the direction of the McSween place. He rode a few paces behind.

Once Ames called back, "You'll never be able to get through to McSween, anyway. The ranchers have his place surrounded."

"Worry about that when we get there," Mulvane told him.

They rode on through the night for nearly an hour, neither man speaking. Then they caught the flicker of firelight up ahead. Mulvane said softly, "Harmon's crew. We'll pull up here."

Ames said, "You figure on walking right through them, Mulvane? What if I give the alarm?"

Mulvane grinned. "They'll shoot the hell out of you, too. You're forgetting that you're a sheepman. These boys came up here to skin all sheepmen."

John Ames sat astride the horse and said nothing. Mulvane dismounted and led the two horses back off the trace. Then he untied Ames' feet and let the sheepman climb stiffly from the saddle.

"What now?" Ames asked.

"Walk," Mulvane told him. He motioned Ames on ahead, and the sheepman started off through the woods, Mulvane behind him, gun in hand. He didn't think it would be too difficult to get through the circle of besieging ranchers and their gunhands. They wouldn't be expecting anyone trying to break through right now.

Moving on through the trees, they gave the camp-fire a wide berth. They had covered about fifty yards of the grade below the McSween ranch when a man suddenly rose out of the brush in front of them.

"Who the hell is this?" he asked suspiciously.

Mulvane laughed. "Put away the gun. I'm looking for Harmon."

"Who's with you?" the sentry growled.

"New hand just came up," Mulvane told him. He had started to push by when the sentry struck a match and held it up to their faces. Catching sight of Ames, he yelled suddenly, "Sheepman!"

Mulvane swung hard with his right fist, driving it into the sentry's stomach, doubling him up and knocking him back into the bushes. "Run!" he yelled at

Ames, and they both started up the grade through the trees, bullets following them as they ran.

They had gone about twenty-five yards when Ames suddenly pitched forward on his face. Pulling up, Mulvane knelt beside him, after firing several quick shots back at the man who had been pursuing them.

Ames, on the ground, was gasping for air. "In the back," he wheezed. "They got me for good, Mulvane. No use staying."

Mulvane could hear the men threshing through the woods and coming toward them. He realized that if he stayed here with Ames he would be a dead man, too.

"I'm done," Ames gasped. "Go on ahead."

Regretfully, Mulvane darted off through the woods, hearing more shots fired after him.

Running up in the direction of the McSween house he heard Jehu McSween calling out, "Hold it up, mister, or you'll be dead."

"Coming in," Cass shouted. "It's Mulvane."

"Hold your fire," McSween growled. "It's that damned fool sheriff."

Mulvane sprinted up on to the porch, past the overturned wagons, and darted in through the open doorway. There were a dozen men inside the house, and many more were outside at the barricades. Some of the men in the ranch house had been sleeping on the floor, but they were all awake when Mulvane came into the room. He caught a glimpse of Charity in the doorway, looking across at him, concern in her eyes.

"What brings you up here at this hour?" McSween asked.

138

"Had a man with me," Mulvane explained. "Lost him on the way up. One of your sheep raisers — and a man who's been working with Griff Bannerman of Circle H."

"Who's this?" McSween asked sharply.

"John Ames," Mulvane told him. "That's the reason he's not here helping tonight."

One of the men in the room said grimly, "Ames didn't come in, Jehu. We sent a man up there to tell him, too."

"Found him with Bannerman," Mulvane said. "They were having a private confab. It's been Ames and Bannerman, all the time, trying to stir up things in these hills so that you and Harmon would go at each other's throats."

"Why?" McSween asked quietly.

"If you go under," Mulvane said, "John Ames will take over your pasture land and become the biggest sheep raiser in this part of the country, just as Bannerman might end up the biggest cattleman if Circle H goes under and he takes Circle H range." He added, grinning, "All you two damned fools have to do is shoot each other up."

McSween stared at Mulvane. Then he said, "Harmon know this?"

Mulvane shook his head. "Not yet. And Harmon will shoot me on sight."

"You figure Ames is dead now?" McSween asked. "We heard the shooting down below."

"Had a bullet in his back," Mulvane told him. "Bannerman's still free."

"Then it's your word against Bannerman's. Why should Harmon believe you?"

Mulvane shrugged. "Maybe he won't, but it's worth a try. Denton doesn't think all of the ranchers are too eager for this fight anyway. They might decide to give it up."

"I'll ask for a parley in the morning," McSween said evenly.

"You can tell him I got a confession out of Ames," Mulvane said.

McSween pointed a finger at Mulvane and said quietly, "I'm not crawling out of this affair, Mulvane. They brought this fight up into my mountains, and they're going to have it, if that's what they want."

"Nobody wants it," Mulvane told him. "If they rush this place tomorrow, there'll be plenty of men killed on both sides."

"You tell Harmon to call off his dogs and I'll talk with him," McSween said.

Mulvane accepted a cup of coffee Charity had brought out for him. He sipped the hot coffee, and then he said to McSween, "You put up a flag in the morning, McSween, and I'll talk to Harmon."

"Your deal," McSween growled, "and it had better be a good one. You give me a tall story about this Ames, and I'll nail your hide to the wall."

Mulvane just smiled at him as he finished his coffee.

CHAPTER
THIRTEEN

They had a heavy guard set for the night, so Mulvane was able to get a few hours sleep before morning. He had had a few words with Charity before rolling into his blanket on the floor. He'd gone back into the kitchen with the empty coffee cup and said, "Your father's a hard man to deal with."

"They had no right coming up here," Charity had told him, her blue eyes hard.

"I'd like to see it settled without any more killings," Mulvane had said. He'd watched her put the cup into a pan of water, and she'd said over her shoulder, "What will you do after this is settled?"

Mulvane had shrugged. "Move on. A man with a gun can always find a job."

"Is there no other way to live for you?" she had asked softly.

"There never has been," Mulvane had said. Then he had gone back to his blankets and turned in.

In the morning McSween raised a white flag, calling for a parley. They were outside, crouching behind the sandbag barricade, which faced the trace up which Mulvane had come on his first visit. There had been sporadic shooting again that morning, but it stopped now as Jehu McSween lifted a broomstick with a white square of cloth attached to it.

Down below in the woods, Boyd Harmon yelled, "You giving up, McSween?"

"Asking for a talk," McSween boomed.

"Take your damned sheep out of these mountains," Harmon shouted back, "and we can talk. I've got fifty men around your place, McSween. You'll be going out of these mountains one way or the other."

Mulvane stepped up beside McSween, who was half revealed now above the parapet of overturned wagons and sandbags. He called down, "We're trying to stop this fight, Harmon. I've got something to say to you."

McSween had stepped out into the open with his white truce flag when the shooting stopped, but, as he did so, a rifle cracked from the woods to Mulvane's left.

Jehu McSween staggered as though he'd been struck with a heavy stone and went down on one knee, still clutching the broomstick in his right hand, but his left hand groping at his chest.

Mulvane leaped out and, with the assistance of another sheepman, managed to drag McSween back to cover. Down below he heard Harmon shout, "Who in hell fired that shot?"

Charity rushed from the house to crouch down beside her father as Mulvane ripped away the bloody shirt. The bullet had gone through the chest high up, near the right shoulder.

"Reckon it was Bannerman fired that shot," Mulvane told him tersely. "He's not anxious for a parley of any kind."

142

Jehu McSween looked at him and shook his head in disgust. "Any way they do it," the big sheepman growled, "it ends up the same way. They knock me down and they have these hills."

One of the men at the parapet yelled suddenly, "They're comin' up, McSween!"

Jehu McSween tried to push himself up, but Mulvane held him down.

"We'll handle them," he said briefly, and then he stepped up to the sandbag barricade. At least a dozen men were coming up the grade, trying to find cover behind trees as they ran.

The guns from the ranch house started to bark, and then the men behind the barricade opened up. Mulvane rested his Colt on top of the barricade, took careful aim and dropped a man as he attempted to sprint from one tree to the next.

He caught a glimpse of Boyd Harmon urging his gunthrowers on, firing a Winchester at the barricade. Bullets were thumping into the bags and whipping by overhead.

Mulvane yelled for Charity to keep down low, and he himself crouched, firing steadily until his gun was empty and then rapidly refilling the cylinder. He looked for Bannerman but didn't see him. Then he threw another shot at Harmon, who had found cover behind a rock outcropping.

Two more Harmon men were hit as they attempted to come up closer to the barricade. Mulvane dropped a third man, using a Winchester he'd picked up when a

143

McSween man had fallen away from the barricade with a bullet through the arm.

Harmon men were firing from farther up the slope, too, but, when a group of the sheepmen and their hired gunhands rushed them, they broke and ran.

Mulvane moved out to the far end of the barricade, convinced now that the only way to stop the fight was to stop Boyd Harmon — and Harmon would not be stopped short of death.

The big cattleman had moved up closer to the barricade, and was now firing from behind the stump of a tree less than a hundred yards from the barricade, urging the others to move in.

Mulvane poked the Winchester between two of the sandbags and waited patiently until Harmon gave him a target. The stump behind which Harmon was concealed was partly rotted at the top, and Mulvane was quite sure that a rifle bullet would go through it if Harmon raised himself sufficiently to provide a target.

Behind him he could hear Jehu McSween growling, "Somebody get me up on the sandbags."

The big sheepman was still lying on the ground as his daughter tried to stop the flow of blood. McSween had been hit hard, and he was going to need help shortly — another reason why the fight had to be stopped.

Harmon had his gun around the edge of the tree trunk, and he fired twice. This time, the top of his black, flat-crowned hat was revealed.

Very carefully, Mulvane took aim at the rim of the stump. Steadying the rifle on the sandbag, he squeezed gently on the trigger. Chips of rotted wood flew up as the slug ripped through the top of the stump, and then Boyd Harmon suddenly stood up. He put one hand on the top of the stump as though he were about to speak, but then he fell, and his body rolled out into the open.

The shooting from below stopped, and Mulvane called sharply, "Why don't you boys give up? You haven't got a chance of breaking in here."

There was silence for some time, and then a man yelled, "Where in hell is Bannerman?"

"Rode off," another man said. "If it ain't his fight, it ain't ours, either."

"McSween asked for a talk," Mulvane shouted. "Come on up."

There was considerable discussion down below before two men appeared in the open and started climbing the hill.

"All over," Mulvane said to Jehu McSween. "They're coming up to talk."

"Saved me a bullet hole if they'd done that in the first place," McSween growled.

Mulvane went over the parapet and walked down to meet the two ranchers. He recognized them as Bludsoe and Tillinger, two men he had met in the Cattleman's Bar.

"What happened to Bannerman?" Mulvane asked.

"Somebody saw him ridin' off," Tillinger growled. He was a short, stubby man with graying hair. His right cheek had been grazed by a bullet, and it was still bleeding slightly.

"Bannerman threw that shot at McSween," Bludsoe said grimly, "after Jehu put up that parley flag."

"Reckon I can tell you why, too." Mulvane told them briefly how he'd found Bannerman together with Ames, and how he'd been bringing Ames in the previous night when the sheepman had been shot down. "He's lying down there in the brush now," he finished. "Bannerman and Ames were trying to ruin every rancher and sheepherder in this part of the country."

"Never liked that damned Bannerman," Tillinger said grimly. "Harmon told us if we didn't put up the fight now, they'd have a hundred gunthrowers in these hills by the end of the month, and it would be too late, then."

"Pull your boys out," Mulvane advised. "If you're smart, you and the sheep raisers in these hills will have a survey line drawn and you'll both keep behind it. I'm sure Denton will help you keep the peace. You're throwing all your money down the drain hiring these guns."

"Four of 'em on my payroll," Bludsoe said glumly. "They ain't earned their keep since I hired 'em."

"Send them all packing," Mulvane said, "and put your money into stock. If you keep to your range, McSween will keep to his hills."

"He hit bad?" Tillinger asked. "Hell of a business firing on a parley flag."

"Have to get him in to town," Mulvane answered.

Bludsoe said quietly, "Tell him we'll have that parley with him when he's back on his feet. If we can both agree to a survey line, the ranchmen will stay on their side."

Mulvane went back to the barricade as the ranchers withdrew. In a matter of minutes they were pulling out, taking with them three dead men and several wounded.

"Fight's over," Mulvane told Jehu McSween. "Ranchmen are willing to draw up a survey line through these hills, if you'll stay on your side."

"We'll stay on our side," McSween snapped. "Always have."

"Not Ames," Mulvane reminded him, "and maybe a few of the others got a little careless, too."

"Keep 'em in line now," McSween growled, "if the ranchmen will stay where the hell they belong." He winced with pain as he spoke, and Mulvane ordered a buckboard rigged up with sacking spread out on the floor so McSween could ride down to Boulder in comparative comfort.

"Where are you going now?" Charity asked as Mulvane threw a saddle on the claybank.

"Figured I'd look up Bannerman," Mulvane told her. "I'm still wearing the star, and he's the man started all this."

Bannerman had pulled out either before or after Harmon had been shot. He could have gone straight out to Circle H or back to Boulder City. Mulvane had decided to look in Boulder first.

"Will we see you in town?" Charity asked him.

"I'll be there," Mulvane told her, and he rode off down the grade.

He looked around the spot where John Ames had been shot but was unable to find his body. This puzzled him. Ames had been hit in the back, and it was unlikely that he could have gone very far, but Mulvane still could not find him.

Frowning, Mulvane wondered if there was a possibility the sheepman could have recovered sufficiently to get back to his ranch house. He tried to pick up a trail of blood, but there was no blood, either. Yet Mulvane was positive he had located the exact spot at which Ames had fallen, claiming that he had taken a bullet in the back.

Mulvane sat astride the claybank, looking down at the ground, and then a slow grin spread across his face. If there was no blood, it meant that Ames had not been hit after all — and he'd used the ruse to make good his escape.

He could have either gone back to the ranch house or, possibly, joined up with Bannerman and returned to Boulder City.

Mulvane turned the claybank unhurriedly in the direction of Boulder. He rode on down the trace, noting where the various ranchers who had been in on the raid had turned off, heading out to their own places. Up ahead of him Charity was driving her father on toward Boulder, with two of the McSween hands accompanying her. They were going rather slowly in order not to jounce McSween too much and start the blood flowing again.

Mulvane caught up with them, looked at Jehu McSween on the wagon bed and then rode on, entering Boulder at about two o'clock in the afternoon.

Several of the ranchers had preceded him in to Boulder and had already told Rog Denton of the fight at the McSween house and of the resultant agreement.

148

When Mulvane went up to the sheriff's room he found Doc Partridge with him, examining the wound. He passed on the word that the physician had another patient coming in shortly.

"Gunshot wounds," Partridge growled. "Doesn't anybody in this town just break a leg or an arm?"

The physician left, and Denton said quietly, "So Harmon is dead?"

"Harmon's dead," Mulvane said. "Bannerman is still alive, and so is John Ames."

"And they'll be looking for you?"

Mulvane shrugged. "What do you think?"

"I'd watch how I walked in this town, Mulvane," Denton told him.

Mulvane smiled. "I watch how I walk everywhere. Anybody seen Bannerman in town?"

"Haven't heard," Denton said. "The ranchers aren't too damned happy about him, either. He'll lay low if he's around."

When Mulvane heard the McSween buckboard rolling in to town, he went downstairs and helped carry McSween into a room the physician had assigned to him. When he came out on the street again he saw Rosslyn Elder coming from the direction of the coroner's, where Boyd Harmon's body had been taken. The girl's face was pale as she stopped on the walk in front of him.

"He's dead," she said slowly.

Mulvane just looked at her.

"And you killed him."

"He was there to kill me and anybody else who opposed him," Mulvane observed. "He knew that when he went up to McSween's."

"If it hadn't been for you, he would be alive."

"You never loved him," Mulvane told her quietly. "If you loved him you would have married him. You wanted to keep what you had; you're not the kind of woman who would marry and give up anything."

"I'll pay you back for this," Rosslyn said slowly. "I want you to remember that, Mulvane. I'll pay you back."

"Everybody's paying me back," Mulvane said.

He walked on back to the hotel, and as he was going in to the dining room he suddenly remembered that the fight was all over and U.P. had still not turned up.

Eating his dinner alone in the dining room, he found himself wondering about Bannerman and Ames again. He was quite convinced that neither man had left the country yet, though both would eventually have to. But now, somewhere in Boulder City or close by, two men were lying in wait to kill him.

As he was eating a boy came in with a telegram and handed it to him. He opened the slip, read it, frowned and then put the telegram in his shirt pocket. Now, as he finished his dinner, he hoped that Bannerman and Ames would not keep him waiting too long.

CHAPTER
FOURTEEN

At dusk Mulvane went up to see Jehu McSween and found the big man resting quite comfortably. McSween had a warning for him.

"You pulled the switch on Bannerman," McSween said quietly. "He'll try to do you in for that, Mulvane."

Mulvane nodded. "Figured I'd watch him."

"Few of my men in town if you need them."

"I'll handle it alone," Mulvane said. "Better that way."

"Watch the alleys," McSween warned. "Right now you'd be damned smart to ride out of here. You're not wearing that star any more."

Mulvane had turned the badge back to Rog Denton on coming in to town, knowing that the range war was over. Now he was on his own again; he could move the way he wanted to.

Charity said to him at the door, "You're doing this out of pride, aren't you?"

Mulvane smiled. "If they're here," he observed, "could I run away?"

"You've done enough. No one would blame you for leaving."

The girl stood by the door watching him. "When you go, Mulvane, don't say good-by."

"That the way you want it?" he asked.

"Yes."

He kissed her gently on the forehead, then, and went out, noting that it was full dark now. He headed up the street toward the Cattleman's Bar and found John Fogarty waiting outside, his derby hat on the back of his head, a cigar in his mouth.

"Bannerman been in town?" Mulvane asked him.

Fogarty shook his head.

Mulvane slipped a five dollar bill in the floorman's coat pocket and said, "Keep an eye out for him. I can't play cards and watch out for a damned bushwhacker at the same time."

Fogarty grinned. "I'll watch for him. Obliged." He paused and said, "There's that sheepman, too."

"What about him?" Mulvane asked.

"Never liked his looks," Fogarty said. "So he and Bannerman had a little game they were playing."

"That's how it shaped up," Mulvane said, went into the bar, had a beer and sat down at one of the card tables with little Dave Shaw from Slash E and two other men.

Shaw said, "Hear you had a little blowout up in the hills this mornin', Mulvane."

Mulvane nodded. "You boys still work for Slash E?" he asked.

Shaw shook his head. "Three of us pulled out on her," he said. "Damned tired o' stickin' our heads up to

152

get shot at. Her beef is scattered from here to hell anyway. Reckon she's finished in the cattle business."

Mulvane didn't say anything. He remembered Rosslyn Elder's threat to him, and he wondered how far she would go in repaying him.

"Miss Elder still in town, Dave?" he asked.

"Ain't seen her," Shaw told him.

Mulvane watched John Fogarty lingering near the bat-wing doors, occasionally stepping inside. Once he paused by Mulvane's chair and said in a low voice, "Got a few friends o' mine keep watchin' around this town, Mr. Mulvane. Bannerman or Ames come in they'll know about it."

Mulvane smiled. "Obliged."

He wondered what Bannerman would do. The Circle H foreman would be in no particular hurry. He was a clever man, a man who laid his plans carefully. Mulvane could not imagine him simply riding into Boulder City, dismounting and walking into the Cattleman's Bar, gun in hand. It was more in his nature to skulk in an alley or hide in an abandoned house with a ready rifle.

Ames was another matter. The sheepman had cool courage. He might not be willing to stand up against as fast a gun as Mulvane's, but he would not run and hide when the lead started to fly.

By eleven o'clock in the evening Mulvane had had his fill of cards. Cashing in his chips at the bar, he moved toward the front door, where Fogarty was waiting for him.

"Everything nice and quiet," the floorman said.

Mulvane stepped out onto the porch and stood in the shadows to the left of the door. From now on he would have to remember to stay out of the light, to walk in the shadows.

"They could of both moved out," Fogarty observed. "Bannerman don't have nothing keeping him in this country any more."

"He's here," Mulvane said, and he watched a rider moving by, the horse, a bay animal, stepping easily.

The night was cool and comfortable, with plenty of starlight. It was only the middle of the week, but quite a few riders were in town, and Mulvane suspected that many of them were hired gunhands who'd been released this afternoon, when the ranchmen had decided to compromise with the sheep raisers. Their part of the fight was over; they owed nothing to Bannerman, and they owed nothing to him. They would watch whatever took place with cold eyes, neither helping nor hindering Bannerman if he came to town gunning for a man.

Mulvane looked up and down the street. With the exception of the lone rider, who now dismounted at a saloon farther up the street, nothing moved. He could hear talk and laughter in the saloons, and somewhere a woman was berating her husband, her voice rising and falling.

On a sudden thought Mulvane decided to pay a short visit to the two wounded men over in Doc Partridge's house.

"Keep your eyes peeled," he said to Fogarty. "I'll be over in Partridge's."

154

"Watch the alleys," Fogarty warned, and Mulvane stepped off the porch, angling across the road toward the physician's home.

He went up the stairs, looking in at McSween's first and finding Charity sitting up with her father, who was sleeping as though drugged.

"How is he?" Mulvane whispered.

"The bullet missed his lung," Charity told him. "He should be on his feet in a month." She looked at him carefully and said, "What about you?"

"I'm still alive."

"Why don't you leave?"

"They'd follow me," Mulvane told her. "I know Bannerman's type."

"Then hide out until Denton's on his feet, or let my father give you a few men to help you."

Mulvane smiled. "My fight. Nobody else in it."

He stepped across the hall, then, to look in at Rog Denton, and found him awake and looking at a newspaper. Denton said quietly, "See you're still walkin' high and mighty."

"Watching my step," Mulvane told him.

"A good way to live long," Denton growled. "You figure Bannerman's in town?"

"Nobody's seen him," Mulvane said, "but he could have come in."

"Why not fort up somewhere and let Bannerman show himself? He's the one pushing the fight."

Mulvane shrugged. "Reckon I don't like to crawl into a hole," he said. "There are people in town watching for him."

"He won't show himself," Denton said grimly, "until he has a gun on you, and then it'll be too damned late."

Mulvane said, "You figure the ranchers meant business when they said they'll keep out of the hills and stay behind that survey line?"

"With Harmon gone they won't make any trouble," Denton said. "He was the hog — and that Elder girl, too." He paused and said, "Where in hell is she?"

"Figured I'd find that out, too," Mulvane said. "She has a room across from me at the hotel."

"Too close," Denton said.

Mulvane smiled. "Reckon I'll lock my doors at night."

He talked a while longer with Denton, glanced through the paper the sheriff had been reading and then left.

Like John Fogarty, Rog Denton said, "Watch the alleys, Mulvane. You're a dead man if he gets a bead on you."

Downstairs, Mulvane paused in the darkened doorway before stepping out into the street and crossing to the hotel. He'd seen Fogarty out on the porch of the Cattleman's Bar, and, since Fogarty had not signaled him, Bannerman had not been sighted in town yet.

At the hotel desk, Mulvane asked if Rosslyn Elder was still registered.

"Checking out," the clerk told him. "Went up to her room to pack right after supper."

"She gone, then?"

156

The clerk rubbed his chin. "Might have gone down the back stairway to load a buckboard," he said. "Didn't see her."

Mulvane went up the stairs from the lobby. He didn't like the thought of that rear stairway. A man could ride in to the stables at the rear of the hotel and come up to the top floor without being seen by anyone below.

There were two lights burning in the corridor on the second floor. Mulvane's room was halfway down the corridor. He noticed that the door of Rosslyn Elder's room was slightly ajar and that the light was out.

Standing outside in the corridor, he listened carefully, knowing that she could be in there with a gun, waiting for him to cross to his own room. It was difficult for him to imagine a woman shooting a man in the back, but he would not put it past Rosslyn Elder. As far as she was concerned, he was accountable for all of her troubles.

He was standing by the doorway when he heard the faint sound from the direction of the rear staircase, the sound of someone coming up very quietly.

Sliding his gun from the holster, Mulvane took a chance and stepped into the darkened room, flattening himself against the wall near the door. He waited for a bullet to rip through him, and breathed a sigh of relief when nothing happened.

Standing by the doorway he could hear a man coming down the corridor, walking softly, pausing at Mulvane's room across the hall. He remembered that he'd locked the door upon leaving it, and he could hear the man fumbling with a key in the lock now. Procuring a key for the flimsy lock would not have been too difficult a matter.

Gun in hand, Mulvane edged closer to the door so he could look out. The man across the hall, less than eight feet from him, was Griff Bannerman. Bannerman had unlocked the door and was now opening it. He had his back toward Mulvane as he pushed the door open slowly. Bannerman obviously intended to gain entry to the room, conceal himself in the dark and then open up with his gun when Mulvane came into the room.

Smiling grimly, Mulvane lined the gun on Bannerman's back. He was about to call to him when Bannerman finally stepped into the darkened room. A gun roared inside Mulvane's room, and Bannerman suddenly staggered out just as Mulvane was stepping from across the hall.

Bannerman had taken a bullet in the stomach. Shock and pain were on his face, but he'd managed to lift his gun from the holster as he stumbled from the room, and he swiveled the gun on Mulvane, now, as he lurched toward him.

Mulvane had no choice. Griff Bannerman was a dying man, but he still carried death in his right hand, and he intended to deal it out.

Mulvane fell to one side and rolled on the floor, firing twice at Bannerman as he did so. Both bullets caught Bannerman in the chest.

As Bannerman slumped to the floor, Mulvane leaped to his feet to face Rosslyn Elder, who was coming out of his room, the gun limp in her hand. Seeing him, she tried to raise the gun, but he was on her in a moment,

158

slashing down with his gun barrel, catching her across the wrist with it and knocking the gun from her hand.

She sat down on the floor, then, moaning with pain and clutching her wrist, and still staring at Bannerman, who was lying face down on the floor, his blood staining the carpet.

Mulvane saw her eyes move suddenly in the direction of the back stairs, which were behind him. Then he remembered that John Ames had not yet been accounted for. If Ames had been down below, he would be coming up now, having heard the shots.

Without looking, Mulvane whirled and fired, aiming deliberately high to avoid hitting the man if it were not Ames, and at the same time to throw him off if it was.

As he leaped for the open doorway of Rosslyn's room, he caught a glimpse of John Ames on the top step, gun in hand. The gun barked as Mulvane moved away. But the flash shot Mulvane had sent at the sheepman had thrown him off, and his first bullet went wide of the mark.

Mulvane fired from the doorway, steadying the gun against the door post. He fired only once. Ames began to sag, and he looked down at the carpet as though trying to work out the pattern.

Ames took two steps forward, and as he did so his gun went off, and the slug gouged through the wood floor, leaving a hole in the carpet. He pitched forward on his face, then, his left hand reaching out toward Griff Bannerman, who had fallen less than fifteen feet away.

Mulvane looked down at the two men, and then he holstered his gun. He walked over to Rosslyn Elder's gun and picked it up.

Rosslyn was still sitting on the floor, head down, sobbing incoherently, and Mulvane looked down at her without pity. She was a broken woman without a man, without cattle, without a future — and she had just killed a man.

Mulvane said evenly, "We could lock you up for attempted murder, but I reckon you'll sweat more on the outside. Go on out to your valley, Miss Elder. It won't be pleasant for you any more."

He went downstairs and, meeting a crowd of men coming up, said briefly, "Get the coroner. There are two dead men on the top landing."

Crossing the street he went up to see Rog Denton. He saw relief come into Denton's gray eyes when he walked into the room.

"You made it," Denton said.

Mulvane smiled grimly. "Miss Elder helped me." Then he told Denton of the fight in the upstairs corridor of the hotel.

Denton thought for a moment after he'd finished, and then he said, "Reckon you can ride out now. You won't feel like you're running."

"I'll be gone in the morning," Mulvane told him.

"Where to?" Denton asked curiously.

Mulvane reached in his pocket for the telegram he'd received that noon, and he handed it to Rog Denton.

"What's this?" Denton asked after glancing at it. "Friend of yours?"

Mulvane smiled. "Did some riding with Red O'Day. He's in trouble and needs a little help."

"What kind of trouble?" Denton asked as he handed the telegram back to Mulvane.

"Rustling," Mulvane said casually. "They got a hanging charge on Red."

Denton scowled at him. "You aim to help a cattle rustler?" he asked.

Mulvane grinned. "This one. Seems Red has been rustling his *own* stock."

Rog Denton just stared at him and shook his head. "Luck," he said. "Reckon you'll need it again, Mulvane."

Charity McSween was waiting for him out in the hall when he came out.

"I — I'm glad you're all right," she said. "I heard about it."

Mulvane nodded. "It's all over."

"I didn't want to say good-by," the girl said, "but now I do."

She stepped up to him and kissed him full on the mouth. Then she stepped back, and Mulvane saw tears in her eyes. She hurried into her father's room without another word. Mulvane went out into the street, frowning.

In the morning he was riding the claybank past the telegraph office when the operator came out, waving for him to hold up. Mulvane pulled up the claybank and waited.

The operator grinned. "Got a wire here for Miss Elder. Figured it might interest you, too, Mr. Mulvane. Signed by a fellow named U. P. Mulvane. Relative?"

"Brother," Mulvane said. "What does he say?"

"Coming here in two weeks," the operator told him. "Reckon that ain't no secret." He paused and said, "You figure on waitin' to see him?"

Mulvane smiled. "Next time."

The operator looked at him, sensing that he was riding on. "Will there be a next time?" he asked.

Mulvane said softly, "Who knows?"